INVESTIGATED

MAYA DANIELS

INVESTIGATED

MAYA DANIELS

By Maya Daniels

Daywalker Series

Investigated

Infiltrated

Instigated

Initiated

Infuriated

Ignited

Vinci Books

vinci-books.com

Published by Vinci Books Ltd in 2026

1

The publisher and the author have made every effort to obtain permissions
for any third party material used in this book and to comply with copyright
law. Any queries in this respect should be brought to the attention of the
publisher and any omissions will be corrected in future editions.
A CIP catalogue record for this book is available from the British Library.
Paperback ISBN: 9781036706722

The EU GPSR authorised representative is Logos Europe, 9 rue Nicolas
Poussion, 17000 La Rochelle, France
contact@logoseurope.eu

Chapter One

"He is cutting through the back."

My partner Aiden growls next to me, his eyes trained on the back of the shifter we've been chasing halfway around town for the last hour. My arms are pumping, the breath coming out in short puffs of steam around my face. On the bright side, it's nice not to feel the chill of early winter. On the other, I can really use a break and get this sucker.

The call came in anonymously that the wolf shifter is seen exiting a witch's house, covered in blood. He is dressed all in black, so it's difficult to see the evidence of it, but I can smell the coppery scent that follows him like an arrow pointed at his head. In the last month, the number of calls has increased, the killings have doubled, and we can barely keep up with it. Adrenaline surges though me, the need to get ahold of him to get some answers pushing me faster than normal. We haven't been able to get one peep from anyone about what is feeding this violence between the species.

Not bothering to answer Aiden, I veer off to the right,

barely missing clipping his shoulder with mine. The last couple of weeks, my depth perception has been shit. I'm lucky if I get my ass in a chair without missing the whole thing and landing flat on my back. But that's a problem for another day. Right now, as I wheeze past homes, jump over fences, and trespass through people's back yards, I need to concentrate on getting this guy. Not because I have something to prove, or for some sort of righteous notion of doing something right. As sad as it may sound, it's because I've screwed up more times than I can count lately, and I'll get suspended if the guy gets away.

Aiden heads off to the left, I'm assuming to try and cut off the shifter from further ahead. The bark of a pissed off dog lodges my heart in my throat, but I'm gripping the wooden planks of the tall fence, already catapulting my body over it. Disappearing behind a two-story home, I see just a glimpse of the guy I'm after, and it propels me faster. Adrenaline rushes through me again, my fingers tingling with the weird energy that has been going to town on me and wreaking havoc on my body.

"Get the guy, Franky. Then think about your messed up life." Huffing under my breath, I zip by an open sliding door, hearing chatter and laughter coming from inside one of the homes.

It must be nice, I think gloomily to myself. *To live a life ignorant of all the ugly that hides in the shadows waiting to pounce on you at any given moment.* I don't begrudge them their innocence. I envy it. It's not their fault I was born as a hybrid creature of the night, something they believe is just a figment of their imagination. And fate, the cruel and wicked witch that she is, couldn't just land me in one of the species. No, my parents had to be the rebels of the supernatural world and mix genes. What was supposed to be a one night stand to scratch an itch ended up with a weirdo like me bumping uglies with the rest of them.

Mixed species are looked down upon in our world. The pure blooded love to say it's because we have a higher tendency to go feral, or turn psychopathic. The truth of it is, hybrids get to have mixed powers from both species, and when they reach their prime, they are more powerful than any pure-blooded creature. They can't control us, so they came up with a way to erase us from our world. Hence, there are not many of us around. I assume that they just kill the product of the coitus before anyone finds out, but I could be wrong. Hell, I am wrong more times than not, and that's why I am running after a shifter tonight. Like that time when I thought a guy was really nice only to find out he was a psycho luring me to his den so he and his buddies could have some fun. Needless to say, he misjudged the situation as well as I did. He died, and I ended up on the radar of Andrius Roberti, the meanest motherfucker of the supernatural world.

And, wait for it…my boss.

I was only sixteen at the time, but he kept me on a short leash, threatening to lock me up or kill me if he felt like it. For years, I was looking over my shoulder, and even under my bed, thanks to him. As soon as I turned twenty-one, he showed up and swept me away into his organization, not giving me the option to gracefully decline, which I had every intention of doing. I even practiced what I was going to say in front of a mirror. It sounded great and quite respectable to my ears, until Andrius showed up and pointed his finger at the open car door waiting at the curb.

The Supernatural Agency for Accord is his baby. He only takes those that have proven their worth in his eyes as part of his team. All of them are pure-blooded, their powers manifested, with years of training under their belts. Everyone is praying before they fall asleep that the Agency doesn't come knocking on their door. Not that it knocks. One agent will show up at your door and give you two options. Either go peacefully or die right there in your granny robe and fuzzy slippers. I'm not really the robe and slippers type, but I'm just saying. He collects the best of the best to keep the order the supernatural groups agreed on.

When the supernaturals decided to out themselves to the humans, all hell broke loose. My world collided with theirs and, from the stories I've heard, it was a blood bath. We are stronger, more powerful, and nearly impossible to kill, but the humans have one great advantage. Their number. They outnumber us a thousand to one and it worked in their favor. The Purge, as they call it, happened, and if we were to stay alive we had to agree to keep in the shadows and not mingle with humankind. Our town was created, protected by wards no one could breach, and the Agency was established to keep everyone here in line. No one leaves this town, apart from a select few. Andrius is as close to a god as anyone can ever get in our world, and his team is as feared and as powerful as him. All of them are legends. He collected the strongest, most powerful warriors.

And me.

Rounding a corner, the stitch on my side pulls me from the trip down memory lane just in time to be able to duck and roll, missing the flying fist to my face. My hip and shoulder take the brunt of the impact with the unforgiving ground as I tumble on the sidewalk, pebbles digging into my palms. Ending up in a crouch, my eyes widen when the sole of a size eleven boot obscures my vision. Jerking back, landing on my ass, I scramble like a crab to put distance between myself and the damn shifter that apparently got sick of running.

Just my luck.

A wicked grin splits his face, his eyes lighting up with the strength of his wolf. Usually, they would be the eyes of a predator prepping itself for a fight. Not this guy. There is a crazed glint in his gaze, something I haven't seen even on a rogue gone feral and lost to his animal side. It almost looks like desperation. It gives me a pause, enough time for his other foot to connect with the side of my head. A burst of colors blooms behind my eyelids from the power he put in that hit. My face scrapes on the pavement, but I'm already pushing up and turning to face him. I regret my decision not to carry my weapons tonight, something this jerk should be grateful for.

"If I knew it was a mongrel chasing me, I would've stopped running a long time ago." His voice is gravelly, more animal than man, and bile rises in the back of my throat when he adjusts his junk.

"Aww, look at you." Sweetness is dripping like honey from my lips. "Such a sweet talker. I bet the ladies love it, huh?"

"Roberti must be desperate if he is sending you after me."

"Or you just suck dude, so he figured that's all you're worth." Shrugging nonchalantly, I eye him for weaknesses. Oh, how I wish I had my daggers. "You think you are the top of the food chain because you killed a witch? Hate to break it to ya, but my guess is no. It just makes you a liability we can't afford."

"I killed no one!" Taking a menacing step towards me, he grinds his teeth. "She was dead when I got there."

"Rightttt!" My hands are tingling bad, and my entire

body is quaking with the need to knock his ass out. "And you were not escaping. You were just going for a night run after having a bath in her blood."

"Exactly." Baring his teeth, he swings at my head again.

I'm ready for it this time, so I block with my forearm, stepping in instead of pulling back so I can come face to face with him. They always underestimate the girl. My tall, thin frame makes them think I'm easily breakable, I guess. Why that happens is beyond me, but I'll take it. Shoving my hand flat on his chest, I send all the pent-up energy zapping through him. His body convulses, his manic eyes rolling to the back of his skull. A scream is ripped from me when claws tear at my skin. The shifter's face starts morphing into his wolf, and with just a second to spare, I push myself off him and stumble back.

Dropping on all fours, a dark gray wolf the size of a pony stares at me from two feet away. The same crazed look is swirling in his eyes, his top lip curling over sharp canines as long as my pinky. Saliva is dripping down his fur, and his sharp claws, one coated in my blood, scrape the pavement as if they twitch with the need for more.

The entire left side of my body feels like it's on fire. My blood is flowing freely, drenching my shirt and pants. The scent of it mixing with the witch's blood still saturating the air around him only makes the wolf wilder. I can see it in the posture of his body, the slight hunch of his back legs, and the pinning of his ears on his skull. He's preparing to pounce. With nothing left but to fight for my life, I place my weight on the balls of my feet, bending my knees slightly and bracing for it.

A horrified scream makes both our heads jerk in that direction. I have never in my life heard a sound filled with so much terror. The blood curdles in my veins. Without a second thought, I bolt in that direction, forgetting all about the beast that is preparing to rip me to shreds, and the reason why I am facing off with a crazy shifter in the middle of a street to begin with. To my shock, the wolf is running parallel with me, loping down the street with his gaze trained in the distance. All my pain and injuries are forgotten together with the fleeting thought that Aiden is nowhere to be found. It all gets lost in the rushing of the blood in my ears, my feet barely touching the ground from the urgency I feel burning in my chest.

Rounding a corner, I skid to a stop. Two shadows twist and twirl around a lump in the middle of the street. A hand reaches toward the sky from the crumpled person on the ground, as if warding off the waving shadows. The wolf next to me releases a sound between a growl and a whine, and its ears go back, flattening on its skull before turning around and disappearing into the night. I can't look away from the scene in front of me to even worry that my suspect is getting away, or what that means for me and my future in the Agency.

The darkness around the shadows is all-consuming, sucking in the light from the lampposts scattered down the street. The eerie silence creates a buzzing in my ears that only amplifies the rushing sound of the blood in my veins. Only my gasping breaks the stillness around me, and I realize too late that I shouldn't stand like an idiot in the middle of the road for anyone to see.

The movement of the shadows stop and although I can't see its eyes or face, if it even has any, I can tell when it turns its attention on me. The short hairs on the back of my neck stand on end, and my fight or flight instincts kick in. My gaze is locked on the lump on the ground, slowly disappearing from view as if being erased from this life like it never existed. The horror of that thought keeps me rooted on the spot, even when everything in me screams that I should run. The lump disappears, and the shadows condense into one before heading straight at me. Heart hammering in my chest, my entire being numbs from the crippling fear that overtakes all rational thought. Keeping my eyes open, I stare at my death, now only inches away from me.

All the air is pushed from my lungs when something barrels at my side, sending me rolling for a few feet. The rough pavement shreds all of my exposed skin while I'm skidding on it, unable to stop the momentum. My head cracks on the sidewalk, the sickening crunch too loud to my own ears. Through blurry eyes, I see the shape of a man looming over me, as if checking if I'm still alive, but I can't see his face or his clothing. I know for certain it's not my partner, the wide shoulders and powerful arms definitely not matching Aiden's swimmer physique. It's all fading rapidly as I taste acid in my mouth. The last thought that rolls through my mind is, *'Shit, the shifter got away'*. But then another thought quickly follows, making me chuckle in my mind. *Andrius can't blame me, because I'm going to be dead.* I lose my fight with consciousness with a smile on my face.

Chapter Two

"She let it get away." Aiden points an accusing finger at me as I purse my lips.

Unfortunately for me, I didn't die. The jerk pointing a thick finger at my face found me on the street and brought me to Andrius before dumping a bucket of water on my head. So, here I am, drenched like a rat after a flood and dripping water all over the expensive rugs covering the floors of Roberti's office. By the reddening of his face, I'm quite positive he does not appreciate it. Neither do I, but I can't tell him that right now.

"What are you, five?" Glaring at Aiden, I poke at the rips on my shirt. "You found me unconscious, dumbass. I didn't let anyone get away. As I said…"

"Yes, we all heard what you said." Clenching his meaty fists, Aiden vibrates from his anger. "Shadows materialized out of nowhere and made something disappear." My unwilling partner does not hide his dislike of me. He never has, as long as I've known him.

"And you think what? I made that shit up because a

shifter got away?" My own anger spikes up at his accusation. He might've taken offence when he asked me out and I laughed in his face. It was one of those foot in the mouth moments for me because I thought he was joking. Apparently, he was not. Immortals hold grudges for a very long time, I'll say that much.

"Enough!" Andrius barks, cutting anymore arguments with just that one word.

Glancing at my boss's face, my heart skips a beat at the intent stare he has trained on me. Dropping my eyes to my feet like my boots are the most fascinating thing in the world, I swallow the panic that's trying to overwhelm me and push aside my need to stare him down in a challenge. Submissive I am not, but neither am I stupid. I fucked up. He is going to kick me to the curb now. It isn't like he hasn't promised that a few times already. This had been my chance to show him I'm at the top of my game and I screwed up more than ever.

My palms are sweaty as I keep ripping at the shredded shirt. Not a trace is left from my injuries. I heal fast, yes, but not this fast. Something happened on that street tonight. Something I can't explain, and even when I try, none of them believe me. Hell, I don't even believe myself, and I was there. And who the fuck was that guy that saved my life? I don't need anyone to give me a rundown of what happened. If he wasn't there, I would've been dead right now. Biting on the inside of my cheek, tasting my own blood, I keep my mouth shut. That's the least of my problems. After being in the agency for ten years, I have no idea what I'll do with my life when Andrius tells me to pack my bags. I don't fit in with the human world, even if I could walk out of the wards. Neither do I fit in with the supernatural one, and those same wards hold me hostage.

"Get out!" The softly spoken words pack so much power that my feet are moving before my brain even registers what I'm doing.

Aiden is out the door so fast I feel a breeze ruffle the short hairs that have escaped my braid around my face. I follow right on his heels, holding my breath. Andrius said get out, but not get out of my building. That's a good thing, right? Mind reeling with where I can make myself disappear until my boss calms down, I reach for the door so I can close it behind me, one foot already out the door.

"Not you, Drake. Get your ass inside and close the door."

I was so close, so damn close to escape I can taste it. Sucking in a deep breath, sending prayers to anyone that will listen, I blow it out slowly as I close the door in front of me and turn to face him. Not daring to lock gazes, I stare at his chin. My boss is a perfect example of an immortal being. His physical appearance, which is stuck in his mid-thirties when most of us reach our prime, can lure the unsuspecting fools into a sense of false security. The smart-pressed suit molds to his large frame like a second skin. Refined features, too perfect to be mistaken for a human, hide a wild, predatory power that will knock your socks off before you can take a breath. A demigod, descendant of Ares, god of war, he makes his ancestor proud with his handsome face, chestnut hair, and deep brown eyes.

"Sit!" he barks, and I almost jump out of my skin.

Lowering gingerly at the edge of the already uncomfortable chair, I sit ramrod straight, still staring at his chin. It's an excellent chin, don't get me wrong, but it's definitely not that fascinating that I keep staring at it. The slight smirk that fleets his face tells me as much. Jerking my eyes to the desk, I grip the sides of the chair so I keep my smartass mouth in check. This is not the time to blurt out the first thing that comes to my mind, a trait I often can't control well. Minutes tick by, the struggle with my panic turning into anger.

"I told you the truth of what happened." Pushing the words through my clenched teeth, I finally meet his gaze. My chin juts out defiantly at his calm perusal.

"The shifter got away. He was your target." Leaning his forearms on the desk, his eyes bore into mine. "I have told you many times. You follow orders, do you understand?"

"You would've done the same thing if you were there." Holding onto my courage with everything in me, I don't look away. "I can still hear the terror in that scream. I have no clue what that thing was, but I've never seen anything like it."

"Where are your weapons?" I was hoping with all the shit tonight he wouldn't notice. I should've known better.

"I did not carry weapons on me tonight." Not wanting to give him time to ask questions, I continue talking, changing the subject. "No weapon I own would've helped tonight. I think whatever that thing is, it's not going to just leave. I can feel that we have a big problem on our hands."

"Shadows, you said?" He searches my face, and I let him see the fear I've been pushing aside.

"Like a shadow." Punctuating that I'm not sure what the hell it is, I force myself to look through the memory closely. "There were two of them before they merged into one. And I could tell when it had its attention on me. Definitely sentient and deadly."

"A mist…" His chocolate-brown eyes narrow, while his deep voice trails off, sending a nervous flutter through my chest that short-circuits my brain.

"And the shifter said he didn't kill the witch, he found

her already dead before the call came in." I have no idea why I poked that bear, and I want to kick myself.

"You had time to chat with it?" One perfectly shaped eyebrow lifts in question.

"If you call him planting a boot in my face chatting, sure." Shrugging a shoulder, my fingers grip the sides of the chair so tight I can hear the wood groaning.

"What am I going to do with you, Drake?" Leaning back in his comfy chair, Andrius folds his fingers over his flat stomach.

"Let me go home to take a shower and get some sleep?" Tilting my head, my vision blurs imagining doing just that. "Some food will be nice, too," I add wistfully.

"I blame this on your mixed heritage." Scowling at me, his lips press in a thin line. "Your powers are clashing, distracting you. This was your last try to prove I didn't make a mistake by giving you a chance. Not even my curiosity on figuring you out can last forever."

"I'm not trying to get my ass out of trouble, Andrius." At his sharp look, I backpedal really fast. "Boss...Mr. Roberti, Sir." Ending it with a groan, I cover my face with my hands. "I'm blowing this up big time." My words are muffled through my fingers.

Roberti grunts, agreeing that I'm only digging a deeper hole for myself. At least he is not quiet. That's when I'm ready to pee my pants, when he says nothing. Removing my hands from my face, I fill my lungs and release the breath I'm holding, slowly locking my eyes on his again. The moment of truth has come, and there is no delaying the inevitable. It's my only chance right now if I want to stay in the Agency.

Honesty.

"Okay, listen." The jackhammering of my heart against

my ribs makes me sound breathless and on the verge of tears. "Three weeks ago, some new power started manifesting. Its bursts of energy come and go as they please, and I can't control it. It makes me zone out at times, not to a point where I have no idea what I'm doing or where I am. It's more like my mind wanders off at awkward moments. It doesn't happen often." I rush to assure him before he tells me to get lost. "But it does happen, and that's the reason I've screwed up a few times. On the bright side, it helps when I use it on anyone. It paralyzes them long enough that they can be incapacitated…if it lasts longer than a few seconds."

"Your mother is a pure-blooded vampire," Roberti says pointedly.

"I didn't notice," I reply dryly by default and bite the inside of my mouth the same second. *What the hell is wrong with you Franky!* I scream at myself internally.

"And your father, a pure-blooded Fae." Andrius narrows his eyes at me again, turning them into slits. "Or so all of you say."

"Excuse me? What's that supposed to mean?" Anger bubbles up inside me just like every time my parents are mentioned, especially after my father was killed.

"These new powers could be coming from his side." His words would've been comforting if not for the calculating look in his gaze while he stares at me like I'm a bug under a microscope. "You should've come to me the moment this happened."

"I thought I had it under wraps." The shrug I give him is not intentional, it's like a twitch my body is making out of my control. "Obviously, I was wrong."

"You are going to go home and stay home"—His eyes

bore into mine, the power punch to obey him almost doubling me over— "until I tell you to come back."

"I just need food, a shower, and a good night sleep. Not necessarily in that order either. I'll be as good as new in the morning." A weight lifts off my chest. He is not kicking me out.

I got excited too soon.

"You are suspended until further notice." My mouth opens to argue my case, but it's left hanging, "Get out!"

I realize I didn't say a word back to him when I'm standing outside the building in front of my bike. Scrubbing a hand over my face, my head hangs down on my shoulders. There is nothing I can do to change his mind right now, so I better head home. Yanking the full-face helmet off the handle, I shove it over my head, slapping the top of it with my palm a couple of times. I push the visor down after I straddle the Ducati, the purring of the beast between my legs not soothing me as it usually does.

"Fuck!" The bike wobbles slightly when I slam my palm on it a few times in anger.

With nothing else left to do and a dread taking residence in my chest, I rev the engine before skidding out of the parking lot like the hounds of Hell are on my tail.

Chapter Three

The chatter is a distant hum assaulting my ears as I stare into nothing above the wall full of liquor bottles at the bar. It has been four days since I got suspended and I think I started going insane inside my one-bedroom apartment. The first two days, I only slept, ate, and then slept some more. Those are a blur, and I think I didn't even take a shower. The third day I got pissed off at myself, so I might've broken a few things when I chucked them at the wall. The hallway might also have a fist-size hole next to my bedroom door, but nobody needs to know about that.

To break the insanity before I destroy everything I own —although I don't own much—tonight I dress up and take myself to Raven's Feather, a pub owned by my friend. My only friend, actually, Daren. He is a mage that wants nothing to do with his kind, so he started his own business in the middle of town. Having to hide what I am doesn't make me a social butterfly, so I usually stay away from everyone. Physical touch is something I find repulsive most of the time. My skin is too sensitive, almost like a magnet sucking in whatever the person is feeling at the moment. Not that anyone will touch me, not if they know I am a hybrid. They'll come for my head.

But not Daren.

We crossed paths while I was angry at the world for being a freak, and he was just as angry for losing the woman he loved. She was a hybrid as well, and when the Mages found out, they had her killed, then branded Daren as a traitor. No one is allowed to hide a hybrid. Well, unless you are Andrius, in which case they all turn to look the other way.

The sigil marking Daren is displayed on top of his left hand like a black stamp. He wears it proudly, which is the main reason I actually spoke to him the first time I saw him. Our mutual dislike of the entitled pure bloods, as well as him not hitting on me, made us fast friends.

As unfortunate or as heart breaking as his fate is, and he loves to tell the story often, it kinda worked out well for him. Not being associated with any species, in particular, gained him quite a clientele and a badass reputation to boot. He does not tolerate any bullshit, and has no problem using his magic on anyone. Everyone is welcomed here as long as they follow the rules.

No killing inside the pub.

That's it. As soon as you leave the door, you're on your own. Luckily, Daren has pretty good wards around the place, so it's kinda safe-ish to get to your ride without a problem. Also having the higher-ups visiting has made it a less likely spot to get murdered. All in all, not bad for a town full of supernaturals running on instinct more than rational thought.

"You want another one, or are you going to milk that one all night?" Daren comes to the corner of the bar where

I'm hugging the beer between my palms like it's my precious.

"You buying?" Lifting an eyebrow in challenge, I chug half the beer down my throat.

"Sure." Smirking, he keeps rubbing the glass in his hands with a rag. "If you tell me why you're more prickly than usual."

"I'm not prickly." My mouth twists in a grimace after I snap at him. "Okay fine, I'm prickly, but when I have a reason to be."

"If you say so." His dark brown hair flops over his forehead, and he jerks his head to move it out of his green eyes. Amusement is dancing in his gaze when my eyes narrow at him. "A beer for your thoughts." He chuckles.

"It's a penny for your thoughts, jackass." Sipping the beer, my attention goes over his shoulder as I look at everyone behind me through the mirrored wall.

"Pennies don't work on you." Still chuckling, he grabs a large, frosted mug, filling it up from the tap.

"Touché, my friend." Pointing my beer bottle at him, my lips twitch, but I can't find enough strength to smile.

Daren slams the mug full of beer on the bar, snatching the now empty bottle from my hand. Leaning his hip across from me, his arms fold over his chest. I know the look on his face, and I'm really not in the mood to talk about my problems, but I can tell he is not going to leave me be until I tell him why I'm sitting here instead of chasing some asshole through the streets of Sienna.

"I got suspended." Daring him to say anything with a glare, I pick up the beer, taking a long gulp, still looking at him over the rim of the mug.

"Shit." All the teasing is replaced with a troubled look in his eyes. "You, okay? How stupid, I know you're not okay."

Lowering his voice, he leans closer to me. "Does it have something to do with the disappearances?"

That gets my attention like nothing else. My gut clenches and a shiver like ghostly fingers runs up and down my spine. The image of the shadows twisting over the body in the middle of the street flashes through my mind's eye. The stupid energy that has been missing for three days surges through me and stiffens my shoulders.

"What disappearances?" I'm watching Daren so intently that his eyes widen and he jerks away from me.

My gaze bobs to the mirrored wall behind him, and I can see why he freaked out. My eyes are glowing on my face like lanterns. A gift from my mother and my vampire side. Total contradiction to my elven features, pert nose, and full bow-shaped lips. The golden skin only adds to the freak of nature that is me.

"Damn it, Franky. I hate it when you do that." Frowning, Daren rolls his shoulders, his black button-down stretching over his broad chest.

"Yes, because I do it just for you." My words are as dry as sandpaper. Closing my eyes, I press my thumb and forefinger on the bridge of my nose. "It's been a stressful few days, Daren. You could even say I'm not in full control of myself."

"No kidding." Mumbling under his breath, he sighs. "You really don't know what's been going on?"

My eyes snap open, looking at him without removing the fingers that are applying pressure on the bridge of my nose. Sometimes I wonder if Daren keeps talking nonsense instead of getting to the point just because he wants to hear himself talk. Too bad for him I'm not in the mood for games tonight. Seeing that I'm just staring at him without saying a word, he comes closer.

"Seven people have gone missing in the last four days." His gaze sweeps the pub before landing on me again. "All random, too. You see them now, and a couple of hours later they are nowhere to be found."

"I'm sure the Agency is on it." Uneasiness claws at my chest and I swallow thickly. I hope I'm telling him the truth.

"Aiden was here yesterday. When I asked him, he glared at me and stomped away." The way Daren is pouting tells me Aiden didn't just stomp away, he must've been an ass, too.

"That's not something that will slip Roberti's notice, Daren. The Agency is on it. I'm sure of it."

"Give me a minute." Daren strides off to the other end of the bar where a feline shifter is waving his empty bottle.

My mind is spinning with what he just told me. Could it be connected? Are the shadows that I saw picking off the people in this town one by one while we all play sitting ducks? More importantly, why did Andrius dismiss me so fast without asking a million questions? If my boss is anything he is anal about details. He wants to know if anyone in this town even breathes wrong. So why ignore what I told him? Suspending me is not strange. It has been coming for a long time. But everything else just doesn't sit right with me.

The stupid energy surges through me so suddenly that I gasp and straighten on the barstool, my forearms pressing hard on the polished wood of the bar. My shoulders stiffen with a pinprick between my shoulder blades and the short hairs on the back of my neck stand on end. Trying my best not to be too obvious, I scan the bar behind me through the mirrored wall that is holding shelves of bottled liquor. Someone is watching me; I know it as I know my own name, but I can't see anyone paying any attention to the bar. When a few minutes pass and I still haven't spotted anyone looking in my direction, I slowly relax. I'm getting too jumpy for my liking.

"Paranoia is the last thing you need, girl." Shaking my head, I lift the mug to my lips.

The slapping of a wet towel on the bar next to me makes me jump, the beer sloshing all over my hand, some of it ending up on my shirt and face. Sputtering and coughing, I glare at Daren while he watches me sheepishly from behind the bar. Too busy coughing out a lung, I imagine punching him in the face, which is what I really want at the moment. Maybe his slightly crooked nose can straighten up that way.

"Jumpy much?" The shaking of his shoulders doesn't match his straight face.

"One of these days, you'll end up dead," I rasp, my throat burning like I've swallowed barbed wire.

"That's not even funny right now." Grabbing a lemon, he starts slicing it. It looks hilarious in his large hands—the same ones I've seen wield weapons like they are an extension of his arms.

I'm not sure if it's because he doesn't want everyone to see us talking, or because he doesn't want me to see the fear that flashed through his eyes before he hid them from me. Either way, I don't care as long as he has something useful to tell me.

"So, who told you about this? Did anyone you know disappear?" Turning sideways, I lean my forearm on the bar, not looking directly at Daren.

He stays quiet for a few moments, and I observe the rest of the crowd. The booths lining both sides of the walls are all occupied. Judging by their body language and the proximity of the way they sit, a few couples are on their first, maybe second dates. Four of the tables are for the wolf shifters, easily recognizable by the bulk of their bodies and the fact that they always sit in a group. The pack mentality is not a joke. Here and there the feline shifters sit on their own, their posture saying they are ready to pounce at any moment. There are a few Fae, and even without their distinct features, you'll be able to spot them because the couple of waitresses that Daren has in this pub gravitate towards them, their magic and allure are very hard to resist. Not that they are trying to stay away from it. And then there are the vamps. The loners of our society are mostly on their own, nursing a glass of wine or scotch, looking down their noses at everyone.

None of them look suspicious, to say the least.

"A wolf shifter came a few days ago, asking about a missing girl from his pack," Daren murmurs behind me. "Said if he can't find information here, he is going to see a witch for a tracking spell."

My heart does a painful thud against my ribs, and my gut flipflops. It may be a coincidence, I tell myself, but I don't believe it even as the thought floats through my mind. There are no such things as coincidences in our world. If it looks like a duck and walks like a duck…and all that other bullshit. I don't mention the wolf shifter I was chasing the night I got suspended. Continuing to scan the pub, my nostrils flare in hopes to keep my heartbeat steady.

"That's one girl. Hardly a call for an alarm. People go missing all the time, and she might've run away with her boyfriend from another pack or something." The words taste bitter in my mouth, and it's not from the beer.

"He said that's the fifth person that has gone missing in the last month from his pack alone." Daren sounds really troubled, so I glance at him over my shoulder.

"You said seven in the last four days." Reaching for the beer, I keep staring at his downturned face.

"That's not counting the other four the shifters are missing." Looking at me through his lashes, I can see lines straining his face. "The Fae are missing a few as well now." Dropping his gaze, he starts piling slices of lemons in a plastic container. "And two of those missing are vamps before you even ask."

"Fuck." Spitting the word, I grip the mug so hard I'm worried it'll shatter in my hand.

"Exactly how I feel about it." Daren walks away, stashing his stupid lemons in a small fridge under the bar. Casually, he saunters back to me, a fake smile plastered on his face in case people are watching us. "I must say I'm glad you got suspended, Franky. It's better to stay under the radar right now."

"Are you insane? The Agency needs all of us if this shit is happening." That's when I notice the fear he's been trying to hide all night coming through loud and clear. "What aren't you telling me, Daren?"

"Rumor has it, all of them were not as pure-blooded as we all believed."

'Well shit!' The glass shatters in my hand, the broken pieces cutting deep into my palm.

Chapter Four

"Allow me," a deep, musical voice that would've been way too tempting if I were human says from behind me.

Twisting my head to look over my shoulder, I'm grateful for the pain numbing my hand. The Fae standing too close for comfort should be illegal. His platinum hair falls over his broad shoulders, covering his pointed ears. Too-blue eyes that can suck your sanity in an instant are trained on my hand, thankfully. The straight nose sits above pink lips, the lower fuller than the upper, that are lifted at the corners in an amused expression. High cheekbones stretch his alabaster skin that looks airbrushed. Even his slightly pointed chin works in his favor. The perfection of his face is only softened by the casual long-sleeved t-shirt and dark jeans he is wearing, but that brings attention to his lithe body and powerful arms and legs that can crush me like a watermelon if he gets aggressive.

You never know with the Fae.

"I'm good thanks." Looking away from him, I pluck the

shards from my palm. "See? It's just a scratch." The gushing of blood that follows my words makes me a liar.

I couldn't care less.

"There are vamps in the place, and we don't want them getting agitated, now do we?" I see his elegant hand with long fingers reach for me from the corner of my eye.

"I said I got it." Slapping it away, I grab the wet towel Daren is holding out to me and wrap it around my palm. "It'll heal in a minute."

When no sound comes from the Fae, and I can still feel the heat of his body standing behind me, I glance back at him. His eyes are narrowed to slits, and his nostrils are flaring. Oh, shit. If he starts swinging here, Daren is going to curse us for a month, and we will end up with a similar fate as the rats eating from his dumpster. The last person to start a fight ended up as a monkey locked in a cage for a week in the middle of the pub. I do not want to push him, friend or not.

"You are one of mine." The Fae pushes the words through clenched teeth. "Do you not know who I am?"

"First of all, I'm your nothing." Getting off the barstool, I face him fully. Letting my tiny fangs poke from under my lip, I smile at him like a fiend. "Second, you know shit about me to come and demand obedience. I don't know who you are and guess what? I don't care. You are in my town so I would be careful who I threaten if I were you."

His eyes widen comically, and his shoulders stiffen, but it's barely perceptive. *Ah, here we go*, I think a second before his shock is about to turn to disgust. Color me surprised when he grabs my shoulder and yanks me away from the occupants of the bar. Shielding me with his body, his panicked eyes snap to Daren, who is watching this weird interaction with his jaw hanging open, hitting his chest. I'm gaping as well, but mainly because this is the last thing I expected.

"Are you mental?" The Fae snarls at me. "Put those fangs away girl or fates help me, I will knock you unconscious and drag your ass out of here."

"Stop touching me." My words are soft, but the energy that surges through my limbs isn't, and it makes the Fae drop his hand, stepping away from me before I even finish the sentence. "Don't. Ever. Touch. Me. Again." Punctuating each word, I watch him squirm. The only reason he still has his head attached to his shoulders is the worry I felt from his touch. The guy is not faking it.

"She doesn't like to be touched." Daren's offhanded comment makes both of us glare at him. He shrugs. "What? I'm just telling him how it is. Plus, you two are getting more attention now than if she was flashing her fangs at everyone individually."

"What family are you from?" The Fae does not want to let shit go.

"Drake." Yanking my arm away from him when he reaches for me again, I snatch the leather jacket I left on the back of the stool. "And I'm out of here. Daren, I'll catch you later. Unfortunately, you have weirdoes in your pub tonight and a no-kill policy. I would've stayed otherwise."

Ignoring the stunned Fae, I slap money on the bar and turn to leave. Daren chuckles, swiping the cash like the pro that he is, but as I'm turning away, my eyes lock on a red, penetrating stare through the mirrored wall. My head snaps in the direction of the far left table so I can see who it is. The feeling I got is the exact same one from earlier when I couldn't find the source of my unease. The breath gets stuck in my lungs when I see the table empty.

"What's wrong?" The Fae is watching the pub, scanning the crowd as well, a line marring his perfect face.

"Franky?" Daren has jumped over the bar and is now standing on my other side, his magic prickling my skin.

"Nothing." Blowing out a breath, I roll my neck. "It's nothing. I thought I saw someone, but I was wrong."

"Someone who? Someone you know?" Daren moves, placing himself slightly in front of me, shielding me with his body. To my horror, the damn Fae does the same.

I bristle.

"Seriously?" Shoving both of them away, I storm off, yelling over my shoulder. "I'm the damn law in this town. I'm the one protecting your stupid assess, not the other way around."

This night couldn't have gone more wrong. I was looking for destruction, something to save me from myself and the mess I find myself in. Instead, the rabbit hole gets more profound by the second, and no matter what I do, everything points me back at the shadow. Daren's words are on repeat in my head as I jump on my bike and bolt out of the parking lot, leaving a cloud of dust and gravel in my wake.

Sienna is nestled just off the west coast in California. The humans in general have no clue that it exists, the wards hiding us in plain sight. It's constant night here, something to do with all the portals being open so creatures like myself can hop in and out through the realm. It's like central station for the supernatural world, although my boss likes to call it our capital. The good thing about being hidden from humans is that it keeps the crazy here. I can't imagine if we had to chase them or look for them around the world. Like it or not, we are all stuck here.

Unless you are a Daywalker.

Any supernatural can become a Daywalker if they pass the trials, attend the prestigious Daywalker Academy, and survive long enough to finish the training with flying colors. Those are far and few between thankfully, so we haven't had the need to start policing the cities where so many unsuspecting lives could be lost. My eyes lift from the road, latching on to the monstrosity of the building sitting high up on the hill, overlooking the town like some tyrant. The energy that's been messing up my life zaps through me, making the bike wobble peculiarly and I almost end up skidding on the street.

My arms burn from the effort to keep the bike from tipping over, and for the rest of the ride, I keep my eyes locked on the road. Buildings, homes, and shops zip by in a blur, my mind emptying from all the stress and worries. At least for this moment, I can just breathe and enjoy the control I have of my bike. As stupid as it sounds, driving at top speed with the wind pressing my leathers to my body is the only thing that has kept me calm since my powers started manifesting. I can't control my life and what I'm turning into, but I can manage this bike and the freedom it gives me.

I'm not sure how long I've been circling the streets of Sienna when I finally release the throttle, and the bike begins slowing down. Taking the turn unhurriedly, I park in front of my building and sit still, just taking it in. Another night of staring at the TV without seeing it awaits me, and I will probably end up stuffing my face with leftovers before passing out on the couch. After the body of my father was found drained of blood and mangled like animals had been feasting on it, I lost the will to do anything else but work. I promised myself and my mother that I would find the one that killed him. Since that day, that's the only motivation driving me. It's easy to tell if you look at my apartment that's barely lived in, or the few things I own. Not counting my leathers, weapons, or my bike.

I was not close to my father, but I knew the guy. We even spent a few days awkwardly staring at each other while trying to make small talk. Neither of us were good at it. Much to my mother's displeasure, instead of playing a dad, my father decided to train me with weapons. She hated it. I, on the other hand, loved it. Not my father, no. He was more like an acquaintance. But I did respect him for the master that he was.

Locking the bike, I place the rune Daren made for me on the seat. A light shimmer of greenish light blinks for a second, encompassing my ride. It has theft protection that will knock out anyone that tries to touch it. Anyone but me, that is. I found a few thugs unconscious next to it at the beginning, which was very unfortunate for them. The word spread around, and now no one goes anywhere near it. I still use the rune, just in case.

My feet feel like they weigh a ton as I climb the stairs to my second story, one-bedroom apartment. With each step, it feels like the boulder sitting on my chest gets heavier and heavier. The fact that there are more like me out there is shock enough. Having someone, or something, picking them off one by one is a whole new level of fucked up. My eyes blur, and I feel dizzy from the torrent of thoughts fighting inside my mind when I push my front door open, shouldering my way inside. Dropping my helmet on the small table at the door, I turn to my living room, and my heart stops.

An outline of a man is occupying the only armchair I own, the streaming moonlight through the window casting his features in shadows. He is sitting stock still, one ankle casually crossed over the knee, both hands resting on the armrests of the chair. The memory of the shadow looming over me on the street plays behind my eyelids, sending shivers down my spine. Numbness takes over my entire body when I see him, but it only lasts a second. All my instincts kick in at the same time, and my knees bend slightly, preparing me for an attack.

"Evening Drake." Roberti speaks casually, like he didn't almost give me a heart attack.

"Damn it, Andrius!" Pressing my hand at the center of my chest, I blow out a breath. "I'll die because of you one of these days."

"Little more jumpy than usual, are we?" Chuckling, he leans forward, placing his forearms on his knees. "I didn't think you had it in you."

"Have what in me?" My ears are still buzzing, the rushing of my blood through my veins sounding like a freight train muffling his words.

"Sense of self-preservation." He says it so matter-of-factly, I'm left gaping at him like an idiot.

"Why are you here?" Ignoring his jab because it hits too close to home, I step deeper inside my apartment. "You're calling off my suspension?" Now, that is something that can get my boss off my shit list right now.

"I have a deal for you, Franky." Lifting himself up, I have to crane my neck to at least look in the direction of his face. For some stupid reason, I didn't turn on the light, so we talk like some creeps in the darkness. Unfortunately for me, my vamp side did not give me superior sight. "I have a mission I would like you to take. If you agree to it, you'll be starting in exactly four hours."

"Okay." The word is out before he is done talking.

I wince.

Maybe I shouldn't sound too eager. I have no life apart from work, but Roberti doesn't need to know that. I should've at least pretended to be thinking about it. Judging by the tilt of his head, he is thinking along the same line as well. Damn it! The silence stretches forever, and my lungs start burning from the breath I'm holding. That stupid energy is rearing its head, but I force it down, waiting to hear him say I'm in. It must be connected with the disappearances. I can't think of anything else that will make Andrius Roberti change his mind.

"We have people missing, and my informants are all pointing at the same place." Shoving his hands in his pockets, he starts walking right at me. "I can't send anyone else because they'll be recognized. I need someone inside, and you are my best bet." His tone implies he is very much not happy about his bet, but I don't give a shit.

"Okay," I repeat, sounding choked up from the adrenaline coursing through me. I'm practically vibrating from excitement.

I'm not suspended. I want to shout from the top of my lungs, but I stay quiet, biting the inside of my cheek.

"Pack your bags." He strides past me, walking out of my apartment. "Be in my office in four hours. And Drake." Stopping just outside my front door, he doesn't turn around. "If you screw this up, you won't be getting out alive."

With those ominous words, he leaves. My knees give out, and I drop a few feet from the still open front door like a rock. Dread pools in the pit of my stomach, but excitement is buzzing through me as well. This is what I wanted, isn't it? If I get this mission right, he will realize that I can hold my own and won't take from me the only life I've known. I'll just have to do my best to get shit done. No distractions and no screw-ups.

"You got this, Franky." I sound a hell of a lot more confident than I feel.

Chapter Five

"You have got to be shitting me!" I burst out while glaring at my boss.

This is so not fucking happening right now. I don't care that this means I'm not going to be suspended anymore. I packed everything I own, which fits inside one duffel bag sadly, and couldn't move fast enough to come here and get my assignment. My plans were made by the time my bike stopped in front of the building of the Agency. I'm going to find out who that man was that saved my life. He knows about those shadows, and he wasn't afraid of them. The thread will start unraveling, and we will nail the fucker that has been killing people right under our noses. My secret hope that it might bring me closer to my father's killer rears its head, reminding me that because of this new development, those plans are now flushed down the toilet.

"I told you she'd fuck it up. Just let me do it. I'll figure out a way to change my appearance." Aiden growls from where he is leaning on the wall of Roberti's office.

"Why is he even here?" Flinging my arm in Aiden's

direction, I keep glaring at my boss. "He is not my keeper. Or do I need his permission to do my job?"

Andrius sits mute in his comfy-looking leather chair, rolling a cigar between two of his fingers. His brown eyes scan my face like he has never seen me before in my life, and I want to scream. This must be some sort of punishment, no matter how much they are trying to convince me otherwise. I need to roam the streets of Sienna to find whoever is killing hybrids indiscriminately on a daily basis. Andrius wants to send me away and isolate me from everyone. It's so not fucking happening.

"They are killing people in this town, Sir." Remembering not to anger him more than I usually do by existing alone, I add sir to my rant. "You sending me away will not solve our problems." A thought hits me like a truck, and I whirl on Aiden. "This was your idea, wasn't it? You can't get your head out of your ass, so you decided to remove me from Andrius's mind by locking me behind those damn gates! It's not going to happen. I'll tell you that right now."

"Sit, Drake." The sound of the rounded clipper zings through the air, chopping out the end of the cigar in Andrius's hand.

Like a petulant child, I plop on the uncomfortable chair opposite my boss. I swear he has these chairs here just to add to the discomfort everyone feels in his presence, like the menacing glint in his gaze is not enough to make all of us almost swallow our tongues. Crossing my arms over my chest, I chew on my lip to stop myself from saying anything. My heart is hammering against my ribs while I watch the lid of the silver Zippo lighter fling to the side and the orange flame come to life. Andrius places the thick cigar between his teeth and, not taking his eyes off me, lights it.

A cloud of gray, white, and silver smoke puffs out,

hiding his face from me. The way it twists and expands reminds me of those shadows, and I swallow thickly in hopes to remove the lump in my throat. My body jerks involuntarily when Andrius pushes the zippo closed, the sound of the metal snapping shut ringing in the silence around us.

"Aiden would've been my first choice for this. If he didn't have the urge to try his luck a decade ago at the trials, he would be the one going now." The leather chair groans when Andrius shifts slightly. You can hear a pin drop. "Alas, he did try, albeit unsuccessfully." I swear there is a smirk on his face, but it happens so fast I'm pretty sure I'm imagining things right now. "So, I'm left with you. I don't like it."

"Don't sugarcoat things on my behalf when you tell me how much you find me lacking." Obviously, the insanity from the last four days is still riding my ass because even when he scowls at me, I keep yapping like an idiot. "Point out all my flaws while you try to convince me to actually go along with this crazy idea."

"Convince you?" It's comical seeing amusement and anger war for supremacy on Andrius's face. "Is that what is happening here?"

"Listen." Rubbing a hand over my face, I slump in the chair. "Even if I wasn't a hybrid, which I would like to remind everyone in this room that I am, we both know that there is no way I'll be able to get in." Locking my gaze with Andrius, I chew on my lower lip for a moment. "No way I'll be able to get in." I'm not sure if I'm trying to convince him, Aidan, or myself when I repeat it.

"If anyone can do it, it's you, Drake." Andrius does not look very happy about saying those words. He actually looks constipated.

I want to laugh.

Not because I find any of this funny. I find it absolutely insane and suicidal. There's a manic, crazy laugh bubbling in my chest right now. Aiden mutters something angrily from behind me, but I can't even get into a pissing contest with him at the moment. It takes all my will power not to let my crazy out and laugh like some psychopath.

"You are reckless and have no instinct for self-preservation." A line forms between Andrius's eyebrows, as if he can't believe he is saying this. Neither can I if I'm being honest. "If anyone can get in, it'll be you."

"We are talking about the Daywalker Academy here." Watching the smoke snake up from the forgotten cigar, I get mesmerized by the twisting and looping line reaching towards the ceiling. "They'll probably kill me before I reach their gates."

Hearing Roberti tell me that his informants have all pointed at the academy when it comes to the killings and disappearances in the last month was like a sucker punch to my chest. As soon as I passed the threshold of his office, he rapid fired the details of his mad plan at me, and my mind is still spinning from it. This damn academy is part of my town, but it isn't. It's like a realm all on its own; ominously staring down at us from its perch on top of the hill. No one goes near it if they value their lives. We know those that stupidly try to get in so they can become a Daywalker. Not many come out alive like Aiden obviously managed to do. Even less graduate their stupid trials and training. None of those that work in it have ever come outside the gates.

And Roberti wants me to go there.

"I have someone on the inside that will help you." Andrius sounds reluctant to divulge this info to me, but my ears perk up at that.

"Help me how?" Nerves are causing bile to raise in my throat. "With the trials, so I can get in?"

"You are worth more to me alive, Drake. I'm not sending you to your death." When I just stare at him, he frowns. "If I want you dead, I'll kill you myself. It'll be more satisfying with all the problems you've caused me."

"I feel the love, boss." Drawling, I ignore the gleeful chuckle from Aiden.

"We know that someone has been visiting the town from the academy." Picking up his forgotten cigar, he relights it, leaning back in his chair. "I have it on good authority that all the comings and goings are monitored very closely there. They keep records of it." His eyes narrow, but I'm not sure if he is judging my reaction or if it's because of the smoke surrounding his head like a cloud and stinging his eyes. Mine are watering from the stench of it. "All I need you to do is get in, find those records, copy them, and get out. You'll have help on the inside, and I'll personally be there when you exit those gates."

"Who's my inside help?" I can't believe I'm asking this question like I've decided to sign my death warrant. "It's not a janitor or something, right? It's someone that can help me get access to what we need?"

"You are really sending her there? I want no part of this!" Aiden snarls and stomps out of the office, slamming the door.

Wincing, I roll my shoulders to get rid of the tension. "He really needs to get laid and get off my ass."

"You did hurt his pride, Drake." Smirking, Andrius leans his forearms on the desk. "Even I know that."

"What? No other female has said no to the mighty Aidan when he asked for a fuck? Seriously?" Biting my tongue as soon as the words are out, my eyes close in hopes that this entire day will just disappear from my memory.

"I think he really cares." My eyes snap open, my jaw hitting the floor at the comment. This is so not happening, the whole "me getting a bit of guy advice from Roberti" thing. It can't be.

"I'm a hybrid, and he is a pure blood. He needs a mate, and I'm doomed from birth to spend my very long existence alone. It's how shit works in our world. Can we change the subject now? You didn't answer my question."

"It's one of the professors in the academy." Reaching to his left, he pulls open a drawer. When his hand comes out of it, there is a thick envelope between his long, calloused fingers. "You need to go to the gate, hand over this enve-lope, and pass the trial. When they let you in, he will meet you on the other side."

"Who is it?" Fear, excitement, and dread are having a party inside my body right now. I didn't live this long because I'm not afraid. It's because of it that I survived. "What is he?"

"I don't know," he says, so nonchalantly that I stare stupidly at him for several long moments.

"Excuse you?" Blurting it out, I can't even flinch when he glares at me, his power blasting me like a tornado. I guess he reached his limit for dealing with my attitude for the day.

Too fucking bad for him.

"We've had correspondence for decades. I did push at the beginning to know his identity, but I was told if I'm not satisfied with simply being informed that channel would close." Scratching his chin, for the first time since I've known him, Andrius looks uncertain. "I stopped pressing.

The information that I'm receiving is too valuable to pass up."

"Does this person know that I'm going there?" If I keep chewing on my lip, I might end up biting it off. My fingers tingle from the energy that comes and goes at awkward times.

"He does." Roberti is daring me to say some smartass comment. I can see it in the glint shining from his gaze.

"This screams like a set up to me." Everything in me rebels at the idea of entering the den of death. "How do you know this is not the person that killed my father? What if it's a set up so they can get their hands on me somewhere you can't do anything to protect me?"

I sound like a scared little girl, and it frustrates me that I have to admit out loud how much his protection means to me. Andrius searches my face for a few moments before his eyes soften, the dark pools of power turning chocolate brown. Pushing off of his chair, he rounds the desk and doesn't stop until his legs hit my knees. Crouching, his large hand slowly and purposely moves towards my arm, giving me time to move away if I don't want contact. I appreciate that he respects my boundaries, so I keep my gaze locked on his.

"If I thought that you were in danger and were out of reach of my protection, there would be no way I'd send you in." His deep voice is soothing, and I remember the times when I was much younger, when he did this often to stop my tantrums. When I was angry at life, at my parents, at everything in general. I've accepted my fate now, but it's still calming to see this side of Andrius again. "I can't give you much more than this, Franky. Just trust that I know what I'm doing and if shit happens that you can't handle, this guy, name or no name, will get you out. That much I can promise you."

"Okay." Taking a deep breath, I blow it out slowly through pursed lips.

"All you need to do is"—Still holding his fingers wrapped around my forearm, Andrius squeezes reassuringly — "get the records and get out. The guy will help with your exit. As soon as you have what you are after, I need you outside those gates. Do you understand?"

"Yes." Cracking my neck, I push out another lungful of air. "I have no desire to be anywhere near those mother-fuckers, trust me. I'll be out of there so fast their heads will be spinning."

"Good." Petting my arm, he stands up and moves behind his desk again. "They'll expect you at the gates in twenty minutes, so I suggest you leave now."

"What? Twenty minutes? Are you fucking kidding me?" Jumping off the chair, I'm already grabbing the duffel I dropped on the floor when I got here. "You're not even going to tell me what the damn trials are about?"

"You work best when you are clueless and under pres-sure." Chuckling, his eyes are glittering with laughter. I want to punch his handsome face. "Now, get lost." Throwing the envelope at me, I scramble to catch it without dropping my bag. "And Drake." When I'm hugging the letter to my chest, glaring at him, he gives me a stern look. "You better get your ass out of there alive, and as fast as you can. You really don't want me coming in there after you."

"Got it." With a sharp nod, I square my shoulders and leave his office.

I can do this.

Chapter Six

"This is an idiotic idea." Jumping off my bike, I grab the duffel, yanking the zipper open and muttering under my breath. "You've done a lot of dumb shit in your life, Franky, but this right here tops the cake."

I stop at the bottom of the hill that will lead me to my doom no doubt, so I can strap on some of my weapons. After leaving Roberti's office, I am so hyped up and freaked out that I don't think of arming myself. Maybe Andrius has a point when he says I have a death wish. I react first and think later. It's quite useful in a life or death situation, but not very smart when you know you're headed into danger but you forget to bring a weapon. To my own embarrassment, I've actually done that quite a few times. Yet another thing to prove my boss knows me better than I know myself.

The new energy streams through my body, causing my hands to tingle, and I almost lose a toe when static electricity makes me drop one of my knives. Jumping back, I save my toe but lose some of my dignity. I'm acting like a child instead of a grown-ass female with years as an agent under her belt. There is a strong desire to blame it on these new powers that are messing me up, but if I'm to survive what's coming, I have to be honest with myself. It's those damn shadows. No matter what I do, I can't stop thinking about it. That and the guy that saved my life.

Who was he?

That's another thing. Every time I think about him, there is this unidentifiable feeling that it's imperative for me to know his identity. He didn't just save my life that night. He also healed me and got rid of the shadows somehow. All that before Aiden found me passed out on the street. A flutter in my belly stills my hands where I'm pushing a dagger inside my boot.

Shaking my head, I push all those thoughts away and straighten up. Looking high up the hill, I can make out the tall towers from the academy sticking out like gnarled fingers pointed at the sky. My breath makes small clouds around my face, the temperature rapidly dropping the later in the night it gets. Rubbing my hands together to bring some warmth to them, I take a deep breath.

"Snap out of the funk, girl." Shoving my braid back inside the leather jacket, I zip it up all the way to my chin. "Get this done and you're golden. No need to worry about being kicked out of the Agency."

The pep talk helps, my heart slowed down from the galloping that it has been doing for the last few days. By some miracle, the crazy energy pulls back, staying just at a distant hum in my chest, and that helps my mind to clear. Straddling the bike, I give the spiked tall towers one last look before placing the helmet over my head. Not wanting to be late, I let the Ducati purr for just a second before taking the road up the hill.

The trees are just a blur around me, getting denser as

the road narrows the higher up I get. The winding path for the last mile or so snakes around in sharp twists and turns, forcing me to slow my bike down. Sooner than I would've liked, I can see the massive iron gates of Daywalker Academy standing like the gates of Hell, abandoned and gloomy, surrounded by high walls and ancient trees.

When I stop, then turn off the bike, I realize that not a sound can be heard here. At the bottom of the hill, the crickets were loud, an occasional hoot of an owl or the chirp of a night bird giving it somewhat of a natural feel. This right here is what I would expect if a predator is stalking the forest around me. *Maybe a predator is stalking the forest.* My mind finds it essential to point out, and goosebumps that have nothing to do with the chill in the air cover my skin.

The way I'm stopped in the middle of the path leading to the academy, it almost looks like I'm having a standoff with the black iron gates, facing them but not getting any closer. My head moves slowly left to right as I scan my surroundings. I'm hoping the night hides me since I'm dressed all in black leather, with a black full-faced helmet covering my head and a black bike, which helps me blend in with the darkness. Not a leaf moves up here. Lifting my visor is the smartest decision I made all night. As soon as the cold night air hits my cheeks, I duck, pushing the bike on one side and rolling off it on the other.

The sound of metal hitting metal is like a gong going off in the silence. Crouched on the ground, my eyes dart around, looking for the owner of the dagger the size of my forearm that got stuck in the dirt almost to the hilt after bouncing off the gate. Opening the visor is the only reason I even heard it sailing through the air in the first place. Luckily, I did, though. Otherwise, the dark steel would've been buried to the hilt in my neck, or maybe even my back.

"Very brave while hiding from sight." There is no need to raise my voice. I know whoever it is they can hear me perfectly. "Some may call you a coward, but I'll give you the benefit of the doubt."

A dark chuckle meant to scare me but only managing to piss me off bounces off the wide tree trunks. I don't get the time to stew in it for long because I hear the second blade coming at me from my back. Dropping flat on the dirt, I wince when I hear it hit my bike. The fucker would've been better off stabbing me with it than messing with my ride. Pushing off the ground, my boots barely graze the path before I flip around and send one of my own daggers in the direction of the coward.

My lips stretch out so hard my cheeks hurt from the smile when I hear the pained grunt. Not giving him enough time to pull my weapon out and recover, I send three more much smaller knives his way in rapid succession. I hear each one of them hit its mark, followed by more grunts of pain. It's unfair that the guy is not vocal, I wouldn't mind hearing him scream. I know it's a guy because, once again, he underestimated me. A female would've been smarter, and probably a vain creature that would like me to see her face before she kills me. It's what I would do. This idiot, though, instead of killing me, thought he was going to play with me for a while.

The joke is on him.

"Halt!"

I freeze in a half-crouch where I am reaching for the dagger in my boot. The deep raspy voice booms from just inside the gates, and my head snaps in that direction, searching the darkness. The moon is not full yet, and there

44

isn't enough of a silvery glow to allow me to penetrate the night. When a branch cracks under a foot from inside the forest, my dagger is in my hand, and I turn sideways just enough so I can have both of them in my sight when they emerge.

"What business do you have here?" the one from inside the gates calls out, his body becoming visible in the moonlight while his raspy voice trails off around us. "Uninvited guests are killed on principle alone."

He is easily six-foot-five, maybe six-foot-six from what I can see. His bald head shines like an ornament in the light of the moon. I can't distinguish his features, but when his head turns to look for his buddy, the coward, I see his long hawk-like nose sticking out. My hand clenches at my side with the need to break it for him.

"Maybe you should check for invitations first, huh?" My words are muffled from my helmet, but there is no way I'm taking it off with these jerks around. "Or do you get off on patting down bodies to check if they were invited?" Tilting my head, I wait until his face is turned my way again. "You do look like a creep who would enjoy something like that."

His hands ball up into fists, and his shoulders bunch up. I can see that if the gate didn't stand between us, he would be on me before I can blink. That same deep chuckle from earlier comes from just inside the trees, raising goosebumps on my arms. What little light reaches that area outlines a muscular body with the gait of a predator, just as I assumed. The yellow glow of his eyes marks him as a wolf shifter, although the way he walks is a dead giveaway of what he is. They don't walk the earth, they prowl.

"Were you?" His tenor sends a shiver of apprehension through me.

"Huh?" Catching a movement from the corner of my

eye, I send the dagger I am clutching in my hand flying through the air, sinking right at the feet of the bold one at the gate. "Don't move buddy. The next one will be between your eyes."

"Invited." The wolf growls, sounding like he is trying not to laugh at his friend.

When I blink at him, my mind draws a blank, and he laughs out loud. I can see my weapons held in one of his plate-sized hands when he stops a few feet away from me, the injuries I inflicted already closing up through his ripped clothing. Now I can see his roguish face, with scruff that's a few days old. Full lips are stretched into a friendly smile, but the glint in his glowing eyes says a different story. He will slit my throat while keeping that disarming smile planted on his stupidly handsome face. The black, long-sleeve t-shirt and pants mold to his body like they are painted over his bulky frame.

"Are you invited or an uninvited guest?" he repeats his question, and I finally snap out of the confusion.

"Invited." Reaching for my jacket, I see the wolf tense up, and I freeze. "Take it easy buddy, I'm just reaching for the letter. It's in the inside pocket of my jacket."

"Buddy?" the bold one from the gate mutters under his breath. "They are sending us insane ones now."

Unzipping my jacket slowly so I don't spook the shifter, I grin at him, not that he can see it thanks to my helmet. "You keep this one in a dog house, huh, only letting him out at night to do his potty." When boldie snarls, the wolf in front of me chuckles. "If he mixed with others, he would know I can hear him."

When my fingers graze the thick envelope, I pull it out, giving the shifter enough time to see it's not a weapon. His eyes widen comically when the cream paper is revealed.

Even the bold guy sucks in a breath, fortunately staying mute instead of spewing more insults my way.

"You are much smaller than I expected," the wolf murmurs, his straight eyebrows pulling low over his eyes. "I thought someone else preceded you here. Franky Drake?" he says my name with uncertainty.

"The one and only, my friend." My voice is still muffled from the helmet, and I debate on taking it off when the shifter pivots on his heel, stalking away from me.

"Come on, we need to get you inside. They are expecting you." My eyebrows hit my hairline when he starts walking with a purpose toward the gate. "I can't believe they sent us a boy."

The last word stops my hand from lifting the helmet off. The idiot thinks I'm a guy. A boy, in his words. Then I realize what might've confused the dumbass. I don't fight in the typical female style, and there is no one better with daggers and knives in all of Sienna thanks to my father. With a name like Franky, I can see how it can be taken wrong.

Deciding to take advantage of the misunderstanding, my hand drops to my side, and I turn to get my bike. Luckily for both of them, there is only a scratch on the paint, and that can easily be fixed. Pushing the visor back down, I roll my ride at the looming, open gate of the academy. If the welcome committee is anything to go by, I might just have enough fun here to forget why I was dreading crossing the iron gate.

"Franky, the boy, at your service," I tell the bold one cheerfully when I walk past him, but he only stares at me with rounded eyes.

I liked him better when he called me insane.

Chapter Seven

My feet falter when I cross the wrought iron gate. There is no mistaking the searing of magic on my skin, a clear indication that the wards placed around the academy are no joke. I feel like my skin is being peeled off with a dull knife and the pain alone forces me to step faster just so I can make it stop. This is some ancient magic, alright. I've never felt anything like it.

Glancing at my two companions, I see that they are not affected by it. Or maybe if guarding the gates is their job, they're just used to it? I have no clue, and no intention of asking, either. As soon as my body crosses over the magic protection, everything around me comes to life. I jerk down, grabbing fast for my bike that I almost drop when the night around me blooms in bright colors.

The wolf stands to the side, watching me curiously, giving me time to gawk at everything around me. Seeing this, if anyone is aware of the beauty hidden behind these gates, I can see why they will be willing to risk their lives to come here. Thanks to the Fae, Sienna is as surrounded by nature as it is urban. None of it compares to what my eyes are looking at now, though.

Tall, red maple trees, their bright red leaves contrasting against the equally impressive cedars and elms, surround a packed-rock path leading to the top of the hill and the still barely visible building of the academy. Wildlife scatters around undisturbed by our presence, some of the squirrels even cheeky enough to dart my way and back, almost as if they want to play. The sky is clear, not a cloud in sight, and the moon looks much closer because of it. Her silvery glow just adds to the enchanting feel around me, causing the breath to get stuck in my throat.

A very strange feeling blossoms in my chest, making me relax and become wary at the same time. It feels like I finally found a place where I belong. Like I've been meant to be here all along. It sinks its clutches into my soul, trying to blend in with me so we are never apart again.

It feels like home.

As soon as that thought hits me, I tense up. Dropping my bike for the second time in one night, my knees bend slightly as I brace for whatever is coming my way. Fingers twitching with the need to hold one of my daggers, I scan the area around me, ignoring the two gatekeepers that are watching me with their heads tilted in confusion. There is magic at play here, and it stinks a hell of a lot like a trap.

"If you are done gawking, we should move along," the wolf says, frowning at me like he can't quite figure me out. "They're expecting you."

Not bothering to answer him, I keep trying to see what exactly set my instincts on overdrive. Everything looks peaceful and beautiful, a little too serene for my liking if I know anything about Sienna. And I know everything there is to know about my town. The colors around me make the white, wide river rocks on the path even brighter, and I follow them with my gaze as far as I can see until they turn to the left, disappearing from view. A slight shimmer in the air, like a light reflecting off a spiderweb, blinks in and out for just a second. Andrius's voice echoes in my head.

You need to go to the gate, hand over this envelope, and pass the trial. When they let you in, he will meet you on the other side.

Roberti said I need to pass the trial before getting on the other side, whatever the hell that means. I didn't hand over the envelope, but I did show it. Now the wolf is taking me to the academy, leaving one thing missing from the instructions given to me. This must be the damn trial. My mouth opens so I can tell the gatekeepers to get lost, but I only manage to fill my lungs with air. A violent shudder under my feet sends me stumbling to the side, luckily catching myself before I end up on my ass. My arms shoot to the side, forcing me to do a great impersonation of a rope walker while I sway with the waves moving the earth under me. As soon as it stops, another loud thump sends me stumbling again. When the sound of a tree snapping booms in the air, my head snaps to the right just in time to see something barreling in my direction, the thick, ancient trees snapping like twigs, making way for it to reach me.

"Fuck this shit!" Anger surges through me, and I throw myself at my bike. Yanking it upright, I jump on the Ducati, revving its engine for just a split second. "They want me to pass a trial? They'll have to catch me first."

The bike shoots up the glowing white rocks like an arrow, my arms straining from the force with which I'm gripping the handles while it jumps over the uneven stones. My body is hunched over the bike, my chest almost pressing over the sleek body. The panicked shouts from the two jerks get lost in the sound of my bike and the crashing of trees, directly followed by a roar that curdles the blood in my veins.

I weave in and out through the narrow road while my heart jackhammers against my ribs and my ears buzz from the rushing of my blood. In no time at all, I can see the sides of the academy peeking through the winding road, and a smile stretches my lips. *Take that suckers*, I think to myself, excitement bubbling in my chest.

"Stick that stupid trial up your asses." Chuckling gleefully, I almost swallow my tongue when two tree trunks, each as wide as a house, slam over the path and block my escape.

Skidding to a stop, my bike fishtails wildly before I manage to take control and stop an inch from hitting the first fallen tree. Not waiting to see what pushed the ancient trunks to prevent me from escaping, I bolt back the way I came. The rear wheel of the bike kicks up a few of the rocks before getting enough traction to catapult me away from another earsplitting roar.

"If I survive this"—My voice shakes, amplified in the confines of the helmet— "I'm going to punch the first asshole that meets me on the other side."

A crazed burst of laughter escapes me.

All my instincts come to life. From the corners of my eyes, I can even see the slight movement of the leaves on the trees. The wild beating of my heart stops before resuming at a slow, steady pace, making everything around me appear like it's in slow motion. All I can hear is the sturdy thumping of my heart.

Thump.

Jerking my bike to the left, I narrowly miss a boulder dropping on the spot where I should've been.

Thump.

Leveling up my ride, I swerve to the right, seeing an arrow zip by my head, disappearing in the night ahead of me.

Thump.

A tree trunk falls a few feet in front of me, obstructing my path. Not slowing down, I brace my legs on the bike and, the moment I'm about to do a head-first collision with it, I push off it, sailing through the air.

Thump.

I tuck and roll over the rocks, pushing off with my hands, not stopping for a second even when I hear the crashing sound of my now-destroyed bike. Veering off, I head through the trees, changing direction yet again and am heading straight for the damn academy. I'm going to get there if it's the last thing I do.

Thump.

A shadow of a body comes at me from my left. Bouncing off the uneven ground, my hands latch onto a branch from a nearby tree, swinging my body in the air before I release it and sail through the forest at high speed. The sound of a body colliding with the trunk of a tree makes me laugh again.

Thump.

Landing in a crouch, my head swings left and right before I see the glint of metal reflecting the penetrating silver rays of the moon through the trees. I feel the blade slicing my shoulder, but I'm already moving, avoiding being hit.

Thump.

Using the trees for cover, I weave in and out, my feet barely touching the forest floor or disturbing the fallen leaves covering it. An owl hoots somewhere above my head before taking a sudden flight, and I drop on the ground, prostrating myself face down. Another arrow flies not an inch above my shoulders. That could've been a clear chest shot. These assholes are getting serious about stopping me from reaching the clearing. Shoving my hands under my chest, I push off the floor and bolt from that spot.

Thump.

My eyes lock on the narrowed gaze of a large feline waiting for me in a crouch. The inky-black fur shimmers like oil in the moon's rays, giving its position away. My hand grabs the blade strapped on my thigh, my hand jerking up and slicing just in time as its massive body pounces on me. Warm fluid covers the skin on my hand when I slice its underbelly, and a pained roar almost bursts my eardrums even through the helmet. The sky opens, and a torrent of rain drenches me from head to toe within a minute.

Thump.

I can see the clearing like a beacon, peeking through the residing forest. Leaving the injured shifter behind, still clutching the bloodied blade in my hand, I push with every-thing in me, heading for that paved area. My shoulder is burning, as are my lungs. The muscles on my legs scream in protest, but the escape of this insanity is so close that I can taste it. It feels like I've been running and fighting for my life for eternity. Mouth dry and breath harshly coming through my parted lips, I fling my body from the forest, landing face-first on the paved front area of the academy, the rain pelting my bruised body and bouncing off the helmet.

Thump. Thump-thump.

The crunching of gravel makes me lift my head up in time to see two shiny black boots stop right in front of my face, raindrops jumping off them like dancing fairies. My eyes close, my body bracing for the kick I'm expecting to receive. When nothing happens, and the sound of shifting clothes reaches my ears, I reluctantly open my eyes to see someone crouching next to me. A curved finger under my chin lifts my head higher, pulling off the helmet from my head. The sharp intake of breath and the headgear dropping like a rock next to him makes me smile. They realized the boy is not really a boy, I guess. With the last of my strength, I look up, and my gaze locks on the bluest eyes I've ever seen.

"Surprise!" I croak before passing out.

Chapter Eight

"This is absurd and unacceptable." The booming voice drags me from sleep.

"I'm sure there is an explanation for all this." The baritone speeds up my heart, coating me like melted chocolate.

Where the hell am I, and who are these people? The question floats through my cloudy mind, disappearing like sand through my fingers when I try to cling to it. I can't remember drinking too much at Raven's Feather, so why do I feel like I'm having the worst hangover ever? The voices keep talking, blending in together like an annoying hum in the background. *It must be the TV.* Assuring myself that I'm just messed up from whatever beer Daren has brewed, I try stretching my arms.

Pain shoots through my entire body, lodging my breath in my throat when a scream is about to escape. Hard, sharp rocks dig into my face when I move, snapping my eyes open. Bolting upright, my head flings wildly as I look around to see where the hell I am. My braid slaps me across the face, and I snatch it, flipping it over my shoulder while reaching for one of the daggers. Seeing the large building in front of me brings all the memories back. At least the rain has stopped. Who knows how long I've been laying here like roadkill.

"Oh, good. She's awake." That same booming voice makes me flinch, my head pounding like a war drum.

"Not thanks to you, that's for sure." Glaring at the large man that spoke, I straighten from my fighting stance. "What the hell is wrong with all of you? That's not a fucking trial back there. It's a death trap!" Spitting the words at him, my fingers are tingling and crackling from the energy surging up with my anger.

The jerk has the decency to lift an incredulous bushy eyebrow at me. I guess not many have the guts to speak to him the way I did, but I'm so angry right now I can literally chew his head off. Roberti is right when he says I work best when I'm clueless or cornered. I'm not exactly sure what happened back there, but whatever possessed me saved my life. One thing I know for sure is that they were not testing me.

They tried to kill me.

"Trials?" Crossing thick arms over his barreled chest, he scowls at me like I'm a child. "You passed no trials girl. I don't know how you did it, but you maneuvered around all of them and just dropped here on our front step."

"It's called survival instinct, asshole. You should look it up." One step towards him is all I manage.

A chuckle sends shivers up my spine, my belly flip-flopping like I'm about to be sick. Very slowly, my head turns in the direction of the sinful sound, my mind screaming that I really shouldn't look. Call it a gut feeling, or a premonition if you will, but that shit is real. It will bite you in the ass if you ignore it, just like I'm doing right now. With all alarms blaring through my head, my gaze locks on bright blue eyes.

The chuckle dies on his full lips, his nostrils flaring up and his square jaw clenching, forcing a muscle to jump on one side of his face. Supernaturals, in general, are beautiful beings. It's just one more weapon in the array of things in our arsenal we can use to trap our prey. Frozen in the prime of our lives, most species are irresistible to humans at least.

Not this guy.

His face is chiseled, so much so I almost feel unworthy to even set my eyes on him. His thick, dark lashes only bring a higher contrast to his bright-blue eyes that shoot daggers at me this very moment. Dark hair surrounds his face, the pale skin standing out harshly against it. If I can describe his face in any accurate way, I might call it deadly perfection. Standing at around six-foot-two, he is slightly taller than my five-eleven, so we are almost at eye level with each other.

Subconsciously, I wipe my damp palms off the leather of my pants, hoping he can't hear the crazy beating of my heart. If the nostrils that flare again are any indication, he cannot just hear it, but he can also smell the insane arousal that hit me the moment we locked gazes. Dressed in a white t-shirt stretching to an inch of its life over his broad shoulders and thick biceps, dark jeans wrapping around large thighs as wide as my waist, and boots I remember seeing before I passed out, he stands there like he expects me to do something. Oh, there are a lot of things that come to mind that I would love to do right now, but none of them are appropriate right here in the open, or sane for that matter. The smirk on his lips reminds me that I'm still gaping at him like an idiot, and I almost jump out of my skin when bushy eyebrows clears his throat.

"Who are you?" he booms at me. I guess he has never heard of lowering the tone of his voice when standing a couple feet away from someone.

"Franky Drake." Reluctantly pulling my eyes away from the sinful temptation still glaring daggers at me, ignoring the sharp intake of breath I'm sure I wasn't supposed to hear, I look at the other man. "Invited guest." Remembering the gatekeepers and their welcoming party, I figure it's better to get that out of the way first. "I have a letter."

Lifting my hands in a gesture of surrender, I keep one hand out, my palm facing him, while very slowly reaching for the zipper of my jacket with the other. I can feel both their eyes like a physical pressure on my hand as it glides the zipper down, then disappears inside my inner pocket. Holding the envelope between two fingers, I slide it out as slow as I can. My body feels like a giant bruise, and I have no desire to test and see if these two know how to fight. Both their bodies look like killing machines, and I could use a break.

As soon as the letter is freed and up in the air, bushy eyebrows strides right at me, snatching it out of my hand. He tears it up angrily, taking all his frustration out on the poor envelope. Flipping the folded paper open with a snap of his wrist, his eyes flick fast through the dark ink lines scribbled on it. The longer he reads, the wider his eyes get, and dread pools in my stomach. *Should I have given this guy the letter? What if it was for the informant Roberti has in the academy?* My teeth are doing a great job of eating through my lower lip as I gnaw on it. Too late to grab it back since he has already read more than half of it. So, I hold my breath and pose myself to kill both of them if the letter is a dooming one.

"Zoltan, mind if you explain this to me?" It takes me a

second to realize bushy eyebrows is talking to the one I'm doing my hardest to ignore.

Tasting my blood when I bite through the skin on my lip, I stifle the groan that is pushing to be freed from my chest. Zoltan walks up, taking the letter from the other guy's outstretched hand, the cool breeze slamming his scent in my face. It's dark and enticing, but I can't exactly put my finger on if it's his natural smell or a cologne he is using. It's not a common thing we do because of all the sensitive noses around, but it is known to happen. Or I'm just deluding myself with ideas to make him less attractive to my stupid body.

"Francesca Drake," Zoltan says with that damn voice, making my skin and nipples pebble like eager fools.

"I prefer Franky, thank you very much." What was supposed to sound sharp and authoritative turned out breathy, and I kind of sound like I am purring like a bitch in heat.

I want to kick myself when he stiffens, his blue gaze flicking to my face before dropping to the paper again. Bushy eyebrows looks from me, to Zoltan, and back with slanted eyes, almost like we are keeping secrets from him. Staring at his face helps get my mind out of the gutter. The longer Zoltan reads the letter, the more I can feel his energy changing, distancing himself from me, while earlier it was like his essence was flirting with mine. It's like a physical blow to feel the cold void gaping between us now, and that clears my head even more.

"Fenrir did say he was expecting her," Zoltan tells bushy eyebrows, turning entirely away from me, like maybe if he can't see me, he can pretend I don't exist.

"Fenrir can go rule his realm and get out of my academy if he thinks the rest of us will bow and grovel at his feet while he entertains guests here like this institution is a joke!" I swear bushy eyebrows grows a few inches when his voice booms in the night, the face getting redder by the second and his body flickering. "I will rip them both apart and be done with it!"

"You cannot stand between mates, Argoz." Zoltan wraps a hand over the pissed off guy, calming him down. "You know this."

When bushy eyebrows, who I now know is called Argoz, calms down instantly, I breathe out a relieved breath. This night keeps getting weirder and weirder, even for my standards. My body sags, telling me I was coiled up from the tension in the air coming from both men. Taking a deep breath, I'm about to thank Zoltan for being levelheaded in this situation before we all end up at each other's throats when his words penetrate my brain.

"Wait, what?" Rushing at him, I grab the letter from his hand, ignoring his growl. "What are you talking about? What mates?"

"See? I knew this was a ploy!" Argoz snaps, getting agitated again, but I ignore him too.

My eyes fly over the text written in a flowing, perfect penmanship. Sure as hell, in it some idiot has written that there is a possibility that Francesca Drake and Fenrir, no last name needed obviously, are mates, and both families request they be allowed to spend one week together. The paper gets crushed in my hands, and it takes everything in me not to let my fangs drop, or my eyes glow. That's another disaster waiting to happen right there.

"It's not a ploy; it's a personal matter that I didn't think would be discussed with the likes of you." Swallowing all the curses and the tantrum I would like to throw, I lift my chin, glaring at Argoz.

"So, it is true?" Zoltan's words feel like he wrapped his hand around my heart and ripped it out of my chest.

Get it together, you idiot! Chiding myself internally, I grind my teeth, avoiding his gaze. Why the hell do I care what he thinks? I'm here to do a job, and I don't know this guy from Adam. For all I know, he is the one killing hybrids all over Sienna.

"Yes." It takes two tries to push that word out, and I feel like I'm about to puke. "I'm here to see Fenrir."

"Francesca!" A musical, too familiar voice precedes the man striding towards the three of us.

"Ah, here comes Fenrir." Argoz growls.

We are still standing just outside of the forest surrounding the academy building. I haven't had a chance to take it all in, the rows and rows of tall windows reaching for the sky, obscuring everything else in front of me. Whoever spoke is hidden behind Argoz's bulky frame, but when the large men move to face the person, I get my first glimpse of Fenrir.

"You!" The word is wrenched from my lips.

Chapter Nine

Argoz's head snaps in my direction, and I stop everything that I wanted to say to the Fae smiling at me like I'm the love of his life. It's the same asshole I met at Daren's bar who offered to help with the cut on my hand. Coincidence?

I think fucking not.

"Should've waited for me at the gates." I continue talking like I didn't just use "you" as an accusation.

"I'm sorry, my dear, the class lasted longer than expected." Fenrir spreads his arms wide, his platinum hair floating around his face like he expects me to fall into his embrace.

Umm, no thanks.

As soon as he is close enough, I stick my hand out straight, stopping him from closing the distance between us. The tips of my fingers poke him in his firm chest, and a slight line forms on his handsome face. Looking confused, he reluctantly reaches for my outstretched palm, and I grab his hand fast, giving it two hard pumps like we just closed a business deal. His frown grows, and Argoz looks like his eyes are about to pop out of his skull.

Zoltan snorts.

"Well, I was almost killed." Smiling sweetly, I hope he can see the fact that I want to separate his head from his body by the look on my face. "In case you were wondering what took me so long to get here."

"She shouldn't even be here." Argoz finds his voice again, unfortunately. "She didn't pass the trials."

"What do you mean I didn't pass them?" Maybe I should go on a killing spree and get rid of all three of them. I can find the records and leave this damn place tonight that way. "I'm standing here, aren't I?"

"I don't know what she did, but she bypassed all of them." He glares accusingly at me, and I glance from Fenrir to Zoltan.

Both of them are watching me with curiosity and suspicion, but I'm tired, pissed off and sore. I have no desire to keep standing here and arguing with all of them. I need a place to hide and think about all the crazy that happened tonight, from the moment I found Roberti sitting in my armchair to the moment Fenrir showed his face in front of me. This is all a mess, and it seems too connected for my liking. I open my mouth to tell them all to get lost, to get them to show me a place where I can wash up and rest, when a loud gong pushes me to my knees.

Squeezing my eyes shut, my hands press over my ears, and I feel a trickle running through my fingers over my chin to my neck. Arms wrap around me, strong and sure, as I'm being lifted in the air and pressed to a firm chest. I can hear sounds around me, faint and distorted like I'm listening to them from underwater. Cold air blasts my face, so I bury my face in the soft fabric of the shirt under my cheek. I know that whoever has me is moving me out of the open, but my body is not being jostled or shook, nor do I feel the person moving at all.

Bright lights eliminate the skin of my closed eyelids, telling me I'm under a roof and no longer exposed to whatever it was that made that horrible sound. For just a moment, a thought about the others and if they are okay floats through my fuzzy brain, but it's gone just as fast. I know one of them is not incapacitated since he is carrying me like a child in his arms. The rest of my senses are dulled to nothing. I can neither smell nor feel anything through my skin where my rescuer is touching me. There is no doubt in my mind that the warm fluid still trickling through my fingers is blood from my ears. The pain is so intense I almost feel numb from it. All I have to do is breathe and hope my eardrums will heal sooner rather than later.

When the person carrying me enters a darkened space and tries to lower me onto what I'm assuming is a bed from the sinking of the soft padding under my body, I release the hold on my ears and clutch their arms like a lifeline. My eyes are still closed, but I'm numb and disoriented from pain. Tasting acid in my mouth, I know if I try to speak I'm going to empty my stomach all over the person that helped me, so a pathetic moan is my argument for them to stay.

I feel vulnerable.

I've never felt like this in my life, and it scares the shit out of me. *You found the perfect place to test your immortality, Franky. Right in the mouth of the beast, you idiot.* My internal voice keeps yapping as if I'm not aware of all that. All my muscles unclench when the safe and strong arms stay wrapped around me. I should feel embarrassed that I'm clinging like a monkey to the guy, but right now, I couldn't care less.

He sits on the soft mattress, folding me in his lap, and I

soak up the false security he offers like a sponge. I can already feel my body mending, the dull hum of the energy in my chest coming to life and pushing through my limbs. With deep breaths, I control it, hoping I don't zap the person holding me to kingdom come with it. The damn thing is unpredictable at the best of times, so I'm not sure what it can do during the times I'm running on fumes. Slowly, but surely, my senses come to life, while the guy still holds me in his embrace, rocking my body gently. To my horror, his scent hits me first, dark and tempting, short-circuiting my brain and lodging a lump in my throat.

Zoltan.

Why the fuck couldn't it have been Argoz that grabbed my pathetic ass to hide me from whatever? My body is already responding to Zoltan's nearness, and I get angrier at myself by the second. Seriously, why can't shit go right for me for once? And what is it about this guy in particular that triggers my inner nympho, that I can't control my body's response to him. I've never had a problem ignoring men before. Not even the Fae can have an effect on me since I'm basically one of them. Well, half, but that's not important right now.

"Shhh…I got you." Zoltan's deep voice vibrates in his chest where my cheek is pressed firmly, like I'm trying to merge myself with him. His large, warm hand rubs my back and arm in smooth, even strokes. "I got you. Nothing is going to hurt you. I won't allow it."

He keeps repeating the same thing over and over, and I listen to him, mesmerized. He is murmuring under his breath, and I get the distinct feeling that he is not aware that he is talking out loud. Keeping my eyes closed because I'm a coward like that, I let him hold me for a long time. Everything around me disappears, all thoughts of pain, investigation, Roberti, murders, and the academy leaving my head.

All I know is the man holding me in his arms, his sinful scent and voice and the safety of his body wrapped around mine. *Just for this once. For just a few moments,* I assure myself as I fully relax and mold to him.

The crashing of a door being flung open and bouncing off the opposite wall makes me bolt upright, the top of my head colliding with Zoltan's chin when both of us jump off the bed like teenagers caught making out. The room we are in blurs around me and I sway on my feet, almost face-planting on the thick rug covering parts of the floor. Strong fingers grab me by the arm, holding me upright while I dangle like a drunk in his grip.

"There you are, thank the fates." Fenrir's voice does not sound musical right now when he reaches for me. He seems worried, and it's grating on my nerves when I bat his grabby hands away.

"Shut up!" The words are slurred because of the tongue that feels too thick for my mouth.

"Why are you here," Zoltan snarls, yanking me closer to him.

Fenrir snarls back.

Great. I feel like a chew toy between two snarling, angry dogs. Crazed laughter bubbles in my chest, but only a pathetic moan can be heard. What the hell is wrong with me? I can feel my body is healed, but I can barely keep my eyes open. Everything is blurry, and my head feels like it's full of cotton.

"I came for my mate." Fenrir snaps at Zoltan, but it's not the sinful guy that gets alert at that. It's me. "I saw you taking her away from the open, and I'm grateful. I will, however, have her back now."

"What…" I bite hard on my tongue when Zoltan drops

me like I've burnt him and my knees give out from under me.

Crumpling on the floor in a heap, I flop on my back, a burst of the psychotic laughter echoing around us. Tears are streaming down my face, but there is nothing I can do to stop it. This whole thing is so insane that I expect to wake up passed out on some crazy brew I've drunk. Both men are staring at me with concern, and that makes me laugh harder.

"You broke her," Fenrir growls at Zoltan, crouching down next to me. "She was sane when I saw her. Prickly, but sane."

"Take your mate and get the hell out of my rooms." There is no infliction in Zoltan's voice, and I stop laughing.

Fenrir lifts me up like a lifeless corpse, my hands and head flopping around while he folds me like a rug and turns for the door. Before we leave Zoltan's room, he stops, the hands holding me tightening around my body like a vice.

"Stay away from her, Zoltan. I do not wish to stand against you, but if you go anywhere near Francesca, you will leave me no choice."

My mind is spinning with what just happened and why Fenrir said that to Zoltan. Was I onto something when I thought that the too-handsome guy might be connected to the murders? Or is this just a pissing contest between two males for a piece of ass. Because as much as I don't like calling myself that, none of them know me well enough for me to be anything else but that. All the blood rushes down south, and they act more animal than man. My heart skips a beat when Zoltan slams the door closed somewhere behind us, rattling the walls. Fenrir doesn't slow down or miss a beat. He keeps striding purposely down the long hallway while I stare numbly at the high ceilings.

What the fuck just happened?

Chapter Ten

Things start off worse than I imagine. While Fenrir carries me to who knows where, I can't help but think that some mage has cursed me recently. There is no other explanation why no matter what I do, everything goes wrong.

I wasn't supposed to bring attention to myself. This entire craziness depended on it, yet I did that very thing from the moment I neared the damn gate. From the day I was born, I was taught a few rules, ones that would help me stay alive. You don't go anywhere near the academy. You never trust any of the Daywalkers. And most importantly, you never, ever cross one of them.

I broke all those in one night.

Bile keeps rising in my throat the more I think about it. As I keep mentioning, reckless is what I am. Stupid, I am not. Not until I agreed to come here. If I'm lucky, they might just kill me now and get it over with. I don't want to think of the other alternatives.

Another door opens while my mind is spinning with

terrifying scenarios and with whatever is still wrong with me. That sound did more damage than I thought because, yet again, I can't gain control over my body, nor can I keep my eyes open. If I stay alive long enough, maybe I'll look into that as well, then hopefully I can send word to Roberti before meeting my end. Judging by the last hour or so, there is no doubt in my mind that I'll be reaching my end here.

"Francesca." Fenrir has stopped moving while I am stuck in my head, his large palm slapping my face gently. "Open your eyes love. Come on, I need to see your pupils."

That comment could've been reasonable considering the circumstances, but panic grips my heart, stopping its beating. Some weird part of me rebels at the thought of allowing the Fae to see my eyes now. It's really idiotic since he already saw what kind of a freak of nature I am at Raven's Feather. Yet, my eyes squeeze tighter, and my response is just another pathetic moan.

"Shit! You really are worse than I thought." Fenrir dumps me on a bed, my body bouncing a couple of times as I hear his rushed footsteps around the room. "This is not good." He keeps muttering under his breath.

A click of a door locking feels like a nail in my coffin.

Bolting upright, I sway again, luckily catching myself on what I assume is a bedpost before I faceplant on the floor. With my eyes still closed, I strain my ears to hear where Fenrir is. Roberti might trust this guy, but the fact he was in town and approached me the same night I ended up here with him sends alarms blaring in my head.

"You are safe with me." Fenrir must've realized what I'm doing. He sounds insulted.

I snort.

"Yes." Slurring, I grip the post tighter, my fingernails digging into the wood. "Said the wolf to the sheep."

"I am not your enemy, Francesca. I agreed to help, in case you have forgotten. That's why you're here in the first place." The arrogance is oozing from his voice. "But we can talk about that later." I hear his slow footfalls approaching, and my knees bend slightly by reflex. He stops. "I didn't think you'd be affected this bad...you need to feed." The last part is added warily.

And I think nothing else can shock me tonight.

"Stay back." I sound a little better, the shock of what he said shaking off the weakness but still rendering me useless. "If...if you get anywhere near me...I'll...I'll kill you."

"I'm not sure you're capable of standing upright for much longer, love." His condescending tone grates on me. "I assure you, you can't kill a fly right now, much less a pure-blooded Fae." Opening my mouth to tell him to fuck off, Fenrir's next words silence me mute. "I'm your only option if you want to survive here. Unless you would like to explain to the rest of them why a Fae needs to feed on blood inside a place that only pure bloods can enter."

Well, fuck me running, as my partner Aiden would say.

The warmth radiating from Fenrir's body seeps into mine. He comes close enough that I can feel his breath on my face while I was stunned by his words. Everything in me tells me to let my fangs drop and rip his throat out, but I breathe through my nose, controlling the urge the best that I can. I might not like him, or trust him for that matter, but what he said is the ugly truth. He is the only one here that knows why I came and what I am.

And just to add to this insane night—one I'm sure I'll remember for the rest of my life, no matter how short it turns out to be—Fenrir leans in, placing his neck with the fluttering jugular under my lips. The scent of rain and forest slam me hard, the wooden post under my fingers groaning in protest from my tightening grip. The Fae must be nuts for offering his neck on the butcher's block without a care in the world. He either thinks I'm a weakling or he is much stronger than I pegged him.

Not like I haven't fed before. Unlike a pure blood, I don't need blood that often to survive, but I'm also a half breed. Unpredictable as they come. That's why Roberti is the only one I've fed from after my stunt with killing seven males in less than thirty minutes. My blood tries to surge through my veins at the memory, but it only manages to sluggishly move around, confirming Fenrir's statement.

I do need to feed.

No wonder I can barely talk. The weakness, dizziness, and the acid flooding my mouth all should've alerted me this will happen. I'm having a lot of firsts tonight. Still, I don't trust myself to sink my teeth in the stupid male's neck. *I need him here.* I assure myself that's the reason I'm not taking his offer, and not because the crazy bloodlust will force my hand and make me kill him.

"Sit." With as much strength as I can muster, I push him away from me. "I'll feed from your wrist."

I don't have to be looking at him to know that confusion is written all over his face. The energy coming off him is as loud as if he said the words himself. My eyes are still glued shut out of my control, and I get the sudden urge to look at myself. Something tells me that the weirdness of this situation is not over yet.

"Do you have…" Swallowing thickly, I try again to push the words out. "I need the bathroom."

Thankfully, Fenrir doesn't question me. Instead, picking me up, he carries me through the room. Keeping my eyes closed doesn't allow me to see where he is going, but the bathroom must be adjacent to his bedroom since he didn't unlock the door to take me there. I understand the reason why he turned the lock in the first place, not wanting anyone to walk in and see me feeding on him. But it still irks me that he feels confident that I have no issues about being locked in a room with him. I'm a skittish animal, as Roberti likes to say. I don't do well in closed places without an exit accessible at all times.

Something the Fae will learn soon enough.

"I will help you," Fenrir says just as he lowers my feet on the floor.

"You will leave." My voice breaks no argument even though it sounds nothing like me.

"You can barely…"

"Leave." Cutting off his argument, I push against his arms. "Now!"

I can tell he wants to bicker, but thankfully he does not. Staring for long moments, his penetrating gaze like a physical presence on me, he reluctantly walks away after taking my hand and placing it on the cold marble so I can keep my balance. I stand in the same spot he put me until I hear a door softly closing behind him. Keeping my eyes shut, I wait for longer than necessary, making sure he actually left and is not standing in the room with me. When no heartbeat can be heard apart from mine, I slowly lift my eyelids.

Bright colors swirl around me in the dark room, forcing a sharp intake of breath. I don't have very good night sight; it's better than a human's but nowhere near what a pure blood will have. Mouth hanging open, my lungs shrivel from the elimination that surrounds everything in the place. A brighter glow pulses around each thing, intensifying the colors. Stranger still, if I look at one thing for too long, it seems like its zooming in closer, and I can tell the smallest details on it. Like a microscopic hairline fracture on one of the tiles in the shower stall. Or the loss of thread on the plush towel folded neatly on the long marble sink I'm holding onto. I'm standing half turned away from the long mirror, taking over one wall, and my fingers are trembling when I shuffle around to face myself.

The same face as always with its unmistakable Fae features greets me. Wisps of blonde hair that have escaped my braid are sticking our every which way around it. My skin is the same golden hue I know too well.

And then there are my eyes.

Anyone who sees my glowing eyes can never mistake me for anything other than a vampire. Combined with my face, undeniable half blood.

But not tonight.

Stumbling back a step, I gawk at my reflection. My shaking hand lifts slowly to my face, the trembling fingers touching the corners of my eyes to assure myself I'm not hallucinating. The amber glow intensifies the same way it always does when my emotions run high. But the pupil? It's long and vertical, and it keeps on shrinking and expanding, giving me glimpses of the pores on my flawless skin. No supernatural has visible pores on their skin.

"What the hell…?" Gripping the counter, I lean in as close as I can to stare at them. "What the fuck is going on?"

It's something to do with this damn place or that horrible sound. It must be. There is no other explanation why I'm looking at the eyes of a snake staring back at me from my own face. Cold sweat dampens my leathers, icy fingers tracing my spine like death himself is taunting me right now. The knock on the door makes me jump a foot in the air, my head whipping in that direction sharp enough to give me whiplash.

"You okay in there, Francesca?" Fenrir's muffled voice kicks up the beat of my sluggish heart.

"Fine." Choking up, I clear my throat. "I'll... be right out. And stop...stop calling me Francesca."

"You need to feed." He points out, pissing me off. Maybe I *will* tear his throat out if he keeps pushing it.

Taking a long, deep breath, I give those freaky eyes one last look. Pushing off the counter, I stumble to the door, yanking it open with my lashes lowered and my gaze on Fenrir's boots. When I stop in front of him, I grab his hand, not giving him enough time to react. Sinking my fangs in his wrist, I pull mouthfuls of his blood, gulping it greedily. He sucks in a sharp breath, his other hand grabbing my shoulder while he leans closer to me. Repulsion crawls over my skin for what I'm doing, but the richness of his blood pushes it away. Nothing tastes as good as pure blood. Smoother than Roberti's, whose blood has a spicy tang just like his personality and his powers, Fenrir replenishes the strength that I've lost. When I've had enough, I keep drinking just to teach the arrogant male a lesson. I would bet my life this will be something he will remember forever.

Fenrir sways in front of me, the weight of his body pressing against me when he drapes over my shoulders. Retracting my fangs, I close off the punctures, shoving my shoulder under his arm. Dragging him across the room, I drop him unceremoniously on the large four-poster bed, grinning like a crazy person at his half-lidded stare.

"Be careful when you offer your blood, love." Sneering the last word, mocking the endearment he gave me, I keep my lashes lowered, hiding my eyes. "It can cost you your life."

To my surprise, the idiot chuckles. Maybe he is crazy, just like everyone else in this damn place. Including me.

Shaking my head, I turn my back on him and head for the bathroom. If I'm lucky enough, my pupils will be back to normal. If not, I'll need to get the hell out of here. There is no way I'll be able to explain that to anyone.

Snake eyes!

I can't even explain it to myself.

Chapter Eleven

Sticking my head out of the slightly opened door, I check the hallway. After assuring myself that I'm back to normal and the stupid Fae is sound asleep, I figure it's the best time to explore this place. Whatever happened will hopefully keep everyone occupied long enough that no one will pay attention to me. Cleaning up my leather pants and jacket the best I can, I can only grimace at my stained top with dirt and blood marks all over it. It's a good thing my jacket survived and can cover it.

The silence stretches on either side of the door, just like the long hallway. Opening it wider, I lean out as far as I can in case I miss someone standing next to the rows of doors on both sides. A gray floor with no decorative rugs and plain white walls meets my gaze. It looks more like part of a military building than the elaborate castle lookalike I saw from the outside.

Maybe you are in a different building.

The thought fleets through my mind as I step out and close the door soundlessly behind me. I won't have much time before Fenrir comes looking for me. Supernatural healing is as useful as it is annoying at times like these. Stepping as softly as I can so my boots don't make a sound, I pick a side and hurry down the hallway. I really must've been out of it when I was carried around not to notice how long it took to reach Fenrir's room. Through a fog, I remember paintings on walls and plush rugs where Zoltan's room was situated. What that says about each of the men is something I'm going to ignore right now.

I almost sprint when I see the tall, arched window facing me. The hallway swerves to the left and right, making my heart pick up a beat. The dullness around me feels depressing, not because I'm some interior guru or known for my talent for color. Everything I own is black for Pete's sake. But the place that I'm emerging from gives me a creepy feeling. Almost like you're given a punishment by being assigned a room in this area.

Another crazy idea I can think about later.

Low voices float to my ears as I near the window, and I plaster my back to the wall. Darting my eyes left and right, I hold my breath the closer they get while I'm looking for a place to hide. Will I get in trouble if they see me walking around without Fenrir? Do I need an escort everywhere I go? It's not like I had an introduction to what's allowed here. The worse that can happen is they'll kick me out, right? *You wish that's the worst outcome.* The snarky voice in my head reminds me that we are not in Sienna anymore. Not really.

"...is the second time in three days," a deep voice continues speaking sharply, keeping up the ongoing conversation that alerted me to their presence. "We must either close the portal for good, which none of us want, need I remind you. Or we throw caution to the wind and make a stand."

His companion grunts something inimical at first that I don't quite catch. "Good luck to you in trying to convince everyone to take a stand now." The nasally spoken words are filled with so much anger my eyebrows hit my hairline. "Even if we do have the strength, we don't have the numbers to be victorious in such a foolish adventure. Unfortunately, we must stick to the plan, at least until we can remove the meddling vampire."

My ears perk up at that, but they are getting so close to discovering me that I need to either run back, which is the stupidest idea, or show myself before they see me snooping in on their conversation. To my relief, they stop walking. Judging by the sound of their voices, they are only one or two doors down from my hiding spot, which is actually in open sight. "Very stealthy, Franky. Keep standing like a lump in plain sight.'

"Did you hear what happened?" The deep voice lowers, followed by the shuffling of feet. "Tonight they allowed Fenrir's mate to enter the grounds. I wasn't there to see it myself, but I was told Argoz was not pleased while Zoltan allowed it to happen. What's next? We'll be housing families and children?" The venom in the last sentence stuns me.

"I wouldn't mess with Fenrir if I were you. The Fae is more peculiar than the rest of them. You don't want him getting in your business if you can help it. I heard he visited the town before she came. I'll wager anything I have he helped her pass the trials."

"You assume he doesn't plan anything. I'm either too paranoid, or you are too naïve. Either way, I have every intention of looking into it before it's too late for both of us." The deep voice says before a door opens and shuts with a bang.

I'm too curious to see at least one of these people to be able to stand still any longer. Pushing off the wall, I walk around the bend in the hall, acting clueless. Gasping, I place a hand at the center of my chest, blowing a breath through pursed lips when I lock gazes with a stunned man. *You are a horrible actress Franky,* I tell myself, even when the guy buys the horrible act I put on.

"Oh my goodness…" breathing faster, I look at him wide-eyed. "You scared the life out of me."

"What are you doing here?" Snapping out of his stunned mode, he narrows his eyes suspiciously at me.

"I was bored, so I figured I'll explore a little while Fenrir rests." Pouting at him, I roll my eyes internally at the stupidity. Do women even act like this? I have no idea how to behave like one. That's very sad.

"You…you… were bored and decided to explore?" Stuttering, he gapes like a fish out of the water.

I blink at him innocently.

"Yes?" Phrasing it as a question, I tilt my head and hope I look as harmless and as clueless as possible. *Please don't pay attention to me being dressed all in leather, like some gangster,* I plead with my mind. "Should I go wait for him to escort me?"

The guy is as tall as he is wide. A head shorter than me, his mop of curly, dirty-blond hair is like a halo around his head. Somewhat handsome, which is expected considering he is a supernatural, his face is the only clear skin that I can see. His arms and legs are covered in swirly black tattoos that disappear beneath the gray t-shirt and black knee length shorts he is wearing. Bulging muscles strain the fabric of his clothing comically. It's almost as if he dressed in a rush in someone else's clothes. His neck looks as wide as my thigh, but none of that is as intimidating as his eyes.

They are fully black.

No pupil, no iris, not even a touch of white surrounding them. They are entirely black like a void. A demon, then. I've seen a few of them in town, plus one of the agents working for Roberti is a demon. But I've never interacted with them enough to know how to deal with this properly. If I remember correctly, they are very finicky about the way you address them and what body language you use.

You should've thought of this before coming here, dumbass. Berating myself is not going to help now, is it?

"Or maybe you could escort me?" Something must've possessed me in that damn forest while I was running for my life. I honestly can't be this idiotic, but I can't stop talking. "I really would love to see the prestigious academy that I've heard so much about. All of you are like heroes among my friends and family."

Never mind that my mother will kill me herself if she finds out where I am, my only friend loathes them more than anyone else I know, and my boss sent me to spy on them. It's a good cover story if I do say so myself. He must've thought the same because his shoulders square off, and his chin lifts slightly up.

"It's not safe right now to walk the grounds outside." Indecision is warring on his face, so I keep smiling sweetly, batting my eyelashes so much you'd think I have something stuck in my eye. "But... I don't see the harm in showing you the inside." His eyes widen even more, like he can't believe he just said that. Neither can I if I'm honest. "If Fenrir wouldn't mind. You Fae are very touchy when it comes to mates."

"Not as bad as vampires, I assure you." Blurting out the

first thing that comes to mind, I audibly snap my mouth shut. I want to slap myself right now, and the demon's eyebrows hitting his hairline tells me I really should've thought more on my response. "Or, so I've heard," I add lamely, taking a step towards him.

The demon stiffens, and the energy starts pulsing in my chest like an eager puppy wanting to play. My fingertips begin to tingle, and I clench my fists, hoping I'll push it down before I do something stupid. Like fry the guy. Good luck explaining that to whoever is in charge here. *And who is in charge here?* Now that's an excellent question. I might not be able to trick Fenrir into giving me a lot of answers since he knows why I'm here, but this guy is fair game. If I keep up the charade, I might learn something that otherwise would've taken days to uncover, if I'm lucky. Being stuck with him for a while doesn't seem like such a bad idea after all.

"Well? What do you say? I really can't stay stuck in a room while he sleeps." Taking another step, I grind my teeth, pushing the energy further down with everything in me. "It bores me to tears, and I hate when I'm crying. I can't seem to stop when the waterworks start."

I might not know much about acting like a woman, but I damn sure know how much men hate crying. It's like a magic word as soon as the demon hears it. He springs into action, pivoting on his heels and almost jogging down another long hallway stretching in front of me. The same gray floors and dull white walls surround us as he keeps waving his hand for me to hurry up. Keeping the pleasant smile on my lips, I grin internally. This was much easier than I expected, and fingers crossed I'll learn something useful in the meantime.

"I will show you the gathering hall," the demon says

over his shoulder, not slowing down. "It's the most impressive thing in the academy. Females love it there." With a sharp nod, he makes his decision while my eyebrow lifts in reaction to his blubbering. "Why they love it is beyond me. I never said I understand females," he mutters under his breath. I'm sure I wasn't supposed to hear that part.

"I'm Franky, by the way." We are almost running down the hall like the building is on fire, but I remember that I don't know his name. Offering mine is a good start, I guess. I'm not sure he'll like it if I say, "hey demon where are we going."

The air is pushed out of my lungs with a loud oomph when he stops abruptly, and I collide with his back. The guy is as hard as a damn rock. I'm sure it would've hurt less if I slammed into one of the walls.

"Franky? As in, Franky Drake?" My heart skips a beat when he spits my name like a curse.

"Yes." Rubbing at my chest after he almost knocks me on my ass, I glare at him.

"You are a female," he says it so accusingly, I almost feel like apologizing.

"Last time I checked, yes." The sarcasm oozing from my words is not lost on the demon.

"We thought you were a male when they approved the entrance." Returning my glare, his massive arms fold over his chest.

"Obviously." Pressing my lips in a thin line, I'm debating if I should just deck him and leave his unconscious ass crumpled in the hallway. "I'm assuming the 'Fenrir's mate' part was lost in your decision making."

"From what we knew, the two are not connected." That statement is as confusing as everything else.

"You mean two people have right of entrance here?"

When his eyebrows lower over his glare, I finally roll my eyes. "If you thought Franky and Fenrir's mate are different people, did you approve entrance to the academy for two people, or just one? Franky Drake"—I point the finger at my chest"—and Fenrir's mate, whoever it may be?"

The demon did a lot of face gymnastics from the moment I laid eyes on him, but none of it compares to the twitching I'm looking at right now. Shock, horror, anger, confusion, and disbelief fight for supremacy, leaving me gaping at him in awe. It's really amazing to watch.

Urgency won.

"I must go!" Turning like a whirlwind, he sprints away, leaving me stunned, my arms and my jaw hanging limply.

The demon moves fast. One moment I see the guy's back, the heels of his runners hitting his ass from the speed he is using. The next, he is gone, and I almost think I imagine him being there. What stuns me more is the fact that he just left me here while he had a stick up his ass earlier for me walking around without someone keeping an eye on me.

"Just add it to the crazy that keeps piling up, Franky." Shaking off the stunned state, he left me in, I take one step forward, then another. "See this as a blessing and go snoop around while you can."

Heading in the direction that the demon took, I can't help but wonder what this means. Does someone else also suspect the academy is behind the disappearances, or do they have more sinister plans? Is Fenrir behind this second person, or does he have no idea about it? The questions keep piling up, and I don't think I'll have enough time to find all the answers.

I didn't even get the name of the demon.

Chapter Twelve

"You shouldn't be up." Zoltan's voice makes me shiver, and I pray that he missed it.

I doubt he misses anything.

Keeping my eyes on one of the weapons displayed like artifacts in the room I find myself in, I ignore his presence. After a few more long hallways and turns, I discovered the arched entrance that separates the academy from the residential quarters. I think. After everything in the last twenty-four hours, I'm not sure of anything anymore.

Wandering aimlessly, I get lost in the grandeur and riches that represent Daywalker Academy. It's a chance in a lifetime for a half blood like me, and to my embarrassment, I can't help but enjoy just being here. I can totally see the appeal it would have—even with the deadly trials, whatever they may be since I apparently skipped them—for pure bloods to be willing to give their lives to attend this place. Not even walking in the daylight among humans can be as rewarding as just standing on these grounds breathing it in.

There is ancient magic and power pulsing like a beating heart in the monstrous building itself.

My heart beats in sync with it.

I lose all sense of time. It could be an hour or a week that I explore the decorated halls, portraits of many Daywalkers adoring the walls and staring back at me with stern gazes. Many stairways curl up on both sides, leading up and down the main building, and dozens of doors stand open that lead to large, auditorium-style rooms with circular rows of seats. Classrooms? Maybe. Tall arched windows allow the silvery light of the moon to mingle with the many lit candles nailed on sconces positioned strategically around the place. It feels like I am walking in an enchanted dream where you are not sure if it'll be something magical, or a nightmare. Just the anticipation for something to happen guides you along. I ignore it all because an invisible rope is hooked at the center of my chest, pulling me this way and that until it brings me here.

To the weapon room.

"You shouldn't be up," Zoltan repeats, much closer to my back than before.

"I shouldn't be many things, yet here we are." Answering him distractedly, my gaze roams the swords, arrows, and maces hanging on the wall.

"Fenrir is not with you." His deep voice vibrates through me, raising gooseflesh along my arms, tightening my belly.

"Last time I checked, we were not connected by a belly cord." Giving him a fast glance over my shoulder, I don't allow my gaze to linger long on the temptation that is Zoltan. "He was fast asleep when I saw him...I'm not sure how long ago was that."

"You feel better, I take it?" The words sound conversational, but I feel his intent stare like probing fingers inside my head.

My energy surges through me, and to my bewilderment, it thrums in my chest like a purring cat. What the fuck is up with that? Pushing the uneasiness aside, I pretend that I'm giving his question serious thought. *Nothing to see here, folks. No one is freaking out or out of their mind.*

"I don't feel like my head is about to split open, or like I wish I would die." Shrugging a shoulder, I move slightly away from him, acting as if one of the weapons has my full attention.

It doesn't.

All my instincts and awareness have zeroed in on him. I only recently met Zoltan, but I have no doubt that he sucks up the attention as well as the oxygen in any place that he graces with his presence. I know he is a pure blood vampire. There is no mistaking his breed even if you are a fool. How old and how powerful he is, that's a totally different story. If I am to guess, I'll say fucking old. Like ancient. Old enough to match the magic of this place. Is he a Daywalker? And is that power blasting out of him amping up? Probably but I can tell he has tight control over it.

"That is good to know." His chuckle sends butterflies into a frenzy in my lower belly.

"Don't you have more important things to do?" Clenching my fists, I dig my nails into my skin in hopes of stopping myself from turning around and kissing him like a deprived person.

It's this damn place messing me up. I know it! No matter what I tell myself, the fact is, Zoltan is a temptation I must resist and avoid at all costs. Only if my body obeys me and my feet move in the opposite direction of him. Which isn't working when I stay rooted to the spot.

"You need an escort to roam the academy." My palms itch to slap the amusement out of his voice. "I see no one here, so I need to keep an eye on you."

"I should've known you are an errand boy around here." Maybe if I insult him enough, he will go away. It's a suicidal plan, but a plan, nonetheless.

"Exactly." My head snaps in his direction at that word, and he smirks at me. "An errand boy at your service, Francesca Drake." Hearing my full name spoken in his deep voice with that slight accent of his, has never sounded that good. The added wink is totally unnecessary, although it has the intended effect of weakening my knees. I get his point loud and clear. There is no way I'll get rid of him.

"I'm not sure Fenrir will appreciate it." Remembering the demon's reaction, I give it a last-ditch effort. "Fae are finicky when it comes to mates." The word "mates" raises bile in the back of my throat.

"Yes, the Fae are." My heart stops at the look he gives me. Numbness spreads from the back of my skull through my limbs.

Zoltan knows.

He knows I'm half blood, and that look tells me I better play along, or death will be knocking on my door a lot sooner than I think. My fight or flight instinct rears up, my body poising to either battle or bolt in the blink of an eye. He renders me useless by reaching a hand and wrapping his long fingers around my shoulder. All the adrenaline drains from me, and I stare at him like a lamb with a wolf's clamped jaw around its neck.

"What do you want, Zoltan?" I hate that I sound scared and timid, but all sorts of scenarios are playing out in my head right now.

"Only to assure the guests in my home are well taken care of." I feel his hand on my shoulder, spreading warmth through me like a brand.

"Your home?"

"Yes." He keeps looking at me, those blue eyes darkening the longer I hold his gaze. "Come." Turning away, he doesn't release me. "I think I can show you something that will help you see that this place is not as bad as your first impression of it. You just had bad timing."

"The story of my life." Murmuring under my breath, I follow him while trepidation churns in my stomach.

"How so?"

"What?" Frowning, I watch his dark eyebrow arch like an arrow pointing up.

"What exactly is the story of your life?" Moving his hand from my shoulder to the small of my back, he guides me out of the weapons room.

I didn't think I spoke loud enough, but he obviously heard me.

Chewing on the inside of my mouth, I wait until we pass two large men dressed in all black tactical gear. With a startled widening of their eyes, their spines straighten when they see Zoltan, who nods at them distractedly while keeping his eyes on me. Who the hell is this guy? A plain black t-shirt and dark jeans hug his torso and muscular thighs, not indicating that he has any authority here. Even the wolf that met me at the gate looked more dressed up than Zoltan.

Unless...

Did he do this intentionally in hopes of putting me more at ease? But to what end? If he is not aware of why I'm here, he has no reason to doubt that I am really a mate to Fenrir. He might not like me being here, but that hardly calls for all the charades and following my every step. Realizing that I still haven't answered his question, I glance at him sideways.

"Bad timing." Waving a hand like I'm swatting a fly, I sigh. "It seems like it's my specialty, to pick the worst timing for everything."

Nodding as if that makes sense to him, he keeps leisurely striding, pulling me along with him. I find everything around the vast space fascinating, doing my best to ignore the man next to me. When that doesn't help, I figure small talk is a good alternative.

"Where did you say we are going?" Avoiding the curious gazes of those we pass, I keep my eyes trained on the paintings and portraits on the walls.

"It's a surprise." There is humor in his voice. "If I tell you, I'll have to kill you."

A tremor rakes my body at those words, making the sound of the blood rushing through my veins buzz in my ears. Was that just a joke or a subtle hint of what's coming? Even with that gut feeling, I can't walk away from him. It's almost like someone else has taken control of my body. A particular portrait catches my eye, the aristocratic face pulling on my subconscious like I should know who it is. My feet are already moving faster, and I crane my neck to look at it for a second longer.

"What type of Fae did you say you were?" Zoltan's question snaps me out of it.

"I didn't." My words are like sandpaper.

Throwing his head back, Zoltan laughs. His shoulders and chest shake from the volume of his voice, and I stumble over my own feet while I watch him, mesmerized. He is too beautiful to watch, and I want to scratch his eyes out for making me feel like an adolescent instead of doing my job. When he stops laughing at my expense, the permanent smirk returns to his face.

"I would take a wild guess and say you're from the Unseelie court." Giving me a once over that sends my whole body tingling as if he physically touched me everywhere, Zoltan tilts his head. "You are too prickly to be one of the light Fae."

"What is it with everyone pointing out that I'm prickly the last few days?" Glaring at him, I start walking even faster. Not that I know where I'm going, but anywhere is better than here. "And not that it's any of your business, but I'm from the Courtless Fae."

Zoltan stops abruptly, his fingers grabbing my jacket and stopping me along with him. Yanking me closer, he gets in my face, his breath fanning my lips. My heart skips a beat from his nearness.

"Keep that to yourself, and never say it out loud here again." Hissing at me, he looks so stern that it takes me a moment to react. When I'm able to think, I shove him away with all my strength.

He doesn't move an inch.

"Get out of my fucking face, Zoltan." He is standing so close that my chest is touching his with each fast breath I take. "You asked, and I answered. Go take your fucked-up personality somewhere else."

Those intense blue eyes drop to my lips, and dizziness makes my body sway towards him. His breathing speeds up slightly as well, and I know the exact moment when he throws caution to the wind and decides to kiss me. I'm not even breathing, dreading it, and wanting it to happen, unlike anything I have ever wanted. His head lowers, the tip of his nose grazing mine. My eyes close on their own accord while I wait to feel his full lips on mine.

"Francesca! There you are!" Fenrir's voice makes us jump away from each other.

Chapter Thirteen

What the hell were you thinking? internally yelling at myself, I watch Fenrir stride towards us, displeasure written all over his face. *You and me both, buddy.* I wish I can say it out loud. Subtly wiping my sweaty palms on my thighs, I lift my chin defiantly. No doubt he will have a lot to say about what happened in his room. I have no intention whatsoever to explain myself to him. He should know what can happen when you offer your neck to a predator.

"Zoltan." Fenrir stops between us, looking down his nose at the other man. It's quite impressive, I must say, given they are both the same height.

"Fenrir." Zoltan smirks, irking me to no end. I have no doubt he knew Fenrir was near when he pulled that stunt. I would've known too if I wasn't so messed up when Zoltan was around me.

"Franky." Pointing the finger at my chest, I blink innocently when they both look at me like I've grown another head. "What? I thought we are saying our names out loud, given we all know each other."

"Is she always like this?" Zoltan's question is for the Fae, but he doesn't look away from me.

"I would take a wild guess and say yes." Fenrir frowns slightly as if judging my sanity.

"You don't know your own mate, Fae?" The glee in Zoltan's voice makes me want to slap him so hard that his pretty head will be spinning for days.

"Not as good as I thought I did, obviously." Fenrir lies smoothly, not missing a beat. "You should've waited for me. You can't walk around without an escort."

Moving slightly, he positions his body in a way that tells me he is ready to protect me if Zoltan is to pounce. Which is stupid, right? The vampire is standing relaxed, his hands in the pockets of his jeans and his blue eyes flicking from me to Fenrir as if he expects something to happen. I'm tired of the crazy with these two. Bumping into Fenrir's side, I move away from both of them, heading in the direction we were going before Zoltan had his nutty persona take over.

"Both of you stay away from me." Throwing the words over my shoulder, I move purposely down the open space. "I've had enough from both of you for one day."

The high ceilings stretch out way above my head. Colorful tiles cover the floors, creating scenes and patterns that are difficult to see when you are standing on them, but no doubt will form a beautiful picture if you look down from the extending railings on the upper floor. If I can't get rid of the two annoying men, I might just do that. Climb up and stare at it until they get bored enough and leave.

People walk around in a rush, some of them carrying piles of books in their hands, others clutching weapons like their lives depend on it. They all give me glances, some curious and others wary, even hostile. Sporting black shirts and pants, a golden emblem adorns the left side of their chest, and all of them match. Men and women alike move with one direction in mind, like they know where they need to be.

Unlike me.

Well, I know where I want to be, but that's not an option right now. I will instead be outside the gates, away from all of this. Or at least in the place the academy keeps their records, so I can get what I need and bolt out of here so fast they'll only see clouds of smoke from my heels. I've never gotten what I wish for in my life. I'm sure it won't be happening now, either.

"Where are you going?" Fenrir falls in step with me, his shoulders stiff and his head straight.

"It doesn't matter." Giving him a glance, I keep walking. "As long as you're not there."

"You haven't rested after what happened." The Fae does not get the hint to leave me alone. "I will take you around later to see more of the building. I'm not sure how you are even standing on your feet."

"Aww, how nice of you to care, Fenrir." My voice is flat, and a muscle jumps in his jaw. "You'll melt me into a puddle from the sweetness."

"Is all this just a big joke to you, Francesca?" Hissing, he grabs me by the arm and drags me into one of the alcoves under the wide stairway leading to the second floor on our left. "Are you trying to get yourself killed, or worse?"

"Stop. Touching. Me." Pushing the words through clenched teeth, I yank my arm out of his grasp. "I don't want to be here anymore than you want me here. So, excuse me if I do my best to find what I'm looking for and go back where I belong."

"You can't enter the archives without my help." His head turns this way and that, making sure no one is around to hear us. "What you will do by flaunting your presence here is get both of us killed."

"You expect me to sit in your room until you are ready to take me out like some pet?" Ignoring the shivers that his words created, I keep glaring at him. "It's not going to happen, Fenrir."

"Roberti promised that you'll follow my lead. Seeking Zoltan out is against everything you're here to do."

"Seeking…" Snorting a humorless laugh, I shake my head. "I seek no one, you idiot. He found me, and I couldn't shake him off."

"He suspects something is wrong." Mumbling to himself, Fenrir surveys our surroundings warily. "I should've taken it into consideration that you'd get his attention given…" Cutting himself abruptly, he flicks his eyes to my face.

"Given what? That I'm a freak?"

A guy carrying a pile of books that look hilarious in his beefy arms walks too close for comfort, his eyes widening when he spots us huddled under the stairway. Fenrir reaches to cup my face in his large hand, his thumb running over my cheekbone like we are lovers, and I stiffen. The Fae's emotions slam into me now that we have skin-to-skin contact, something my jacket prevented when he dragged me here. Anxiety, excitement, and most of all, crippling fear turn me into a statue unable to push him away. Good thing, too, since a knowing look glints in the book guy's eyes and he smiles like he knows a secret right before he walks away. Fenrir's quick reaction saved us a lot of trouble in the long run, but that's the least of my worries right now.

"You are afraid." My words are so soft they are almost just a breath passing through my lips. "For me, or for yourself?"

His perfect face turns entirely towards me, his gaze searching as if debating if he should tell me the truth. Or maybe if my question is sincere and not just another jab at him. I can't say I blame him; I'm not very friendly on the best of days.

"For both of us, Francesca." My feet shuffle uneasily at the intent look he keeps on me. "Things happened here, things behind closed doors, that only a handful were privy of from the start of the academy. But not like this. Never like this." Taking a deep breath, his nostrils flare. "Something is happening, and I have a feeling if we don't stop it, it'll be the end of us all. That is why I agreed to stick my own neck out and bring you here."

"You've been helping Roberti long before this." Numbness spreads from what he is saying, but I know that's not all of it. He is hiding something, and when his hand drops from my face, my suspicions are confirmed. He knows I can feel his emotions through touch.

"Not like this." Taking a step away from me, he rolls his neck. "I just want you to know that if I had any other choice, I would've never brought you here."

"You didn't bring me anywhere. I walked up on my own two feet." Which is not entirely true. Instead, it's more like I faceplanted here on my own. Chewing on the inside of my mouth, I try to read between the lines of what he is not saying, but I come up empty. "I agreed to be here. And just so we are clear, I might be centuries younger than you, but I'm not a child. I'm a grown ass woman, and you have no need to feel responsible for me or my actions. This is my job, it's what I do. I knew the consequences and the danger that came with it the day I agreed to work for Roberti. Being here is no different."

"Oh, but that's where you are wrong." His shoulders

curve in, his body language aggressive enough to spark up the energy inside me to life. "This *is* different. So much that I'm no longer sure that any of us will live long enough to see it through."

"Then stop wasting time, Fae." Clenching my teeth and my fists, I have to force myself not to punch his perfect face. "Instead of yapping here, show me where the damn archive is so that I can do my job. The sooner I get what I need, the faster I'll be out of here."

"If only that were true." Taken aback by the comment, I'm sure he doesn't realize he speaks out loud, and I can't understand the sadness that flashes through his eyes. "Let us go to the dining hall. It's time for breakfast, and you'll be able to observe those that attend this prestigious place like a good mate should do when visiting the workplace of her lover."

"What do you do here, anyway?" Ignoring the comments on mates and lovers, mind spinning from the weird conversation, I don't protest when he leads me out from under our hiding place.

"I teach Energy Manipulation and Phantasmagoria." The pride is unmistakable in his voice.

"Phanta-what?" That was definitely a mouthful.

"Phantasmagoria." Grinning at me, he winks. "Illusion Crafting."

"Of course you do." Fenrir laughs at the grimace on my face.

Fucking Fae.

Chapter Fourteen

I stay quiet as we walk across the vast, open entrance of the academy. It looks like everyone starts here before splitting up and heading towards whichever classroom or auditorium they need to attend. While we were under that stairway, it seems like the place came to life. My body clock is telling me it's time for bed, which means it's morning. Sienna functions on a night schedule. I should've known since we are at Daywalker Academy, they'd be doing the exact opposite.

Reaching the other side, the hallway splits in two directions. On our right, people rush, and the chatter is a constant buzz bouncing off the walls. A total opposite of the hallway leading to our left. Silence is thick there, but the plush runaway rug and golden accents gets my attention immediately. Pulling me in like a siren call, my feet answer it instantly, moving on their own because they are eager to be there.

"This way." Fenrir's voice is strained when he grabs my elbow, dragging me none too gently to our right. "Snap out of it, Drake." The venomous hiss clears my head of the fog, and my eyes snaps to look at the Fae.

"What the fuck was that?" Keeping my voice as low as I can, I give a strained smile to those around us.

"Later," is all he says, weaving in and out of clustered groups of students.

They are all in different age groups and from different species. It's so strange to see them like this. In Sienna, they live among each other, but they never mix. Each breed sticks to their own, coexisting with the rest by ignoring their presence. Here, all supernaturals are mixed in different groups, chatting heatedly or cheerfully, even slapping each other's backs like best friends. My eyes are blinking fast, as if that will change what I'm seeing. This place might host a murderer, but I must say it has done some fantastic things for all the others.

Enjoying the good that I see in front of me dies a sudden death when the demon I came across during the night points an accusing finger at me from all the way across the long hallway. Next to him stands Argoz, my not so big of a fan. Groaning, I rub a hand over my face. It's too much to ask for an hour or two without drama around here. My brain is shutting down thinking it's time to sleep, and I really can't deal with this right now.

"Want to tell me why Argoz looks like he is about to burst a blood vessel?" Fenrir mumbles, his fingers digging into my elbow.

"I might've met the demon last night when I was wandering the hallways."

"Might?"

"I don't know his name; he didn't give it before running away like a little bitch. Plausible deniability."

"That's not how things work here." Digging his fingers

harder into my elbow, he drags me faster at the oncoming tornado that is Argoz.

"Watch and learn, Fenrir." Taking a deep breath, I grin at a pissed off Argoz. "Watch and learn."

"Miss Drake!" Argoz shouts, even before he is close enough to be heard—that is unless your sense of hearing is enhanced. It's too loud in the hallway. "This is unacceptable behavior."

Pretending I'm deaf, I smile at him wider and even add a little shy wave of my fingers. Argoz's face gets even redder, and he barrels through people, pushing them out of his way like bowling pins. Next to me, Fenrir looks like he is about to either turn around, bolt, or get an aneurism.

"The two of you will be placed in a cell." Stopping in front of us, Argoz seems to grow in size. "Fenrir, you will answer for your plotting against this institution, and she"— A thick finger pointed directly at my nose trembles in anger. My eyes cross to look at it— "will die for daring to step foot here."

"Be careful who you threaten, Argoz." Fenrir's voice is so soft and calm, it sounds more terrifying than the idea of dying here by Argoz's hand. "Unless you can back your claims, I would choose my next words wisely."

"You tricked the Board into allowing two outsiders in our land. The punishment for that is death, as you well know it." Either the energy around Argoz is glittering, or the horror of the situation is making me see things while I stare mutely at the two men.

The demon glares at me with arms crossed on his chest. At least he is wearing clothes that fit him now. The pleasures of small blessings are marvelous.

"I have done no such thing, and I can prove it." Releasing my elbow, Fenrir positions himself slightly in front of me in a protective stance. At this very moment, I don't mind that at all, even if it hurts my pride. "If the Board is looking for someone to blame their incompetence on, they are knocking on the wrong door. A wrong door that can cost them greatly for their threats."

"We have the requests, Fenrir. No need to keep up with the lies."

"Let us see them, Argoz." The smile on Fenrir's face is the most dangerous one I've ever seen as his eyes start glowing slightly.

Oh shit, oh shit, oh shit…

Panic almost makes me start running in place and flapping my hands like a crazy person. The Fae is about to explode, and all of us will be the collateral damage if he unleashes his power in the closed-up space. I know because I might only be half blood, but when the energy uncontrollably explodes out of my body, I destroy half of my apartment. And it is always just a small surge up in my sleep. This is bad. Like really, really bad.

"I signed my request in blood, Argoz." Fenrir takes a menacing, measured step forward. "Let us see the requests, I say."

Argoz deflates slightly at those words, confusion clouding his face. A frown pulls his eyebrows low over his eyes, scrunching up his features. My own fingers are tingling, the tension in the air and the power coming of off Fenrir triggering my own into a circular current coursing through my veins. The air is so thick it's difficult to take a full breath. Ignoring the stares from those around us, a slight movement pulls my attention to the demon that was standing to the side until now.

Two black horns push out through the halo of blond curls around his head. His features sharpen, the bones on his face extending in sharp angles and long claws bursting from his fingertips. What is only a split second seems like long moments to my eyes, and the frantic beat of my heart slows to barely perceivable thumps. The demon springs into action, his body heading straight for the Fae with claws extended for the jugular. My own body reacts, that weird feeling like something else is controlling it overtaking my mind.

Thump.

Shoving Fenrir by his shoulder, I send him stumbling a few steps like he weighs nothing. Turning to face the demon at the same time, my knees bend, lowering me in a crouch, and my right hand pulls back before pushing my hand forward with my fingertips pointed at him. At the last moment, my palm turns, connecting to the center of the demon's chest with such force that the energy churning in my middle bursts from it and I feel his ribs break into pieces under my hand. His body folds inward, flying back so fast it hits the wall and goes through it, sending brick and plaster all over the place.

Thump.

From the corner of my eye, I see Argoz's body flicker, grow, and his human shape disappears like it never existed in reaction to the power that is still swirling around me with a mind of its own. Well, I'll be damned. Argoz is a ghoul. Of course, he won't be something easily defeated, especially given his attitude from the moment I laid eyes on him. Long arms that end in bony fingers with sharp nails stretch way past his knees. Springy hair falls over his thin shoulders from a few places on his otherwise bald skull. A too-wide mouth gapes open with a few rows of razor-sharp teeth, and his soulless eyes focus entirely on me. He transforms from one second to the next, and I don't slow my momentum.

Pivoting in my crouch, placing one hand flat on the cold floor, my leg shoots out and connects with Argoz's caved in stomach, sending him barreling back the way he came.

Thump.

Everyone around us is frozen in various degrees of chatter, laughter, or wide-eyed looks, kind of like time has stopped. Fenrir is standing where I pushed him, eyes closed and palms facing me, murmuring under his breath while his platinum hair is floating with a mind of its own around his face. Argoz bounds up in my direction, recovering too quickly for my taste. His long arms stretch out, grabbing for me. Jumping up, I take hold of one arm and twist it around, dislocating his shoulder, and my head rings from the piercing screech coming from his mouth.

Thump.

He reaches his other hand for Fenrir. the Fae is with his eyes closed, unaware of the danger he is in. Yanking harder on Argoz's bent arm, I fling him like a rag doll and send him through the hole in the wall I made with the demon. As his body sails through the air, one of the sharp nails catch me on the side of my face, the razor like hooks parting my skin like butter. Releasing the arm I'm clutching, I send Argoz away from us, my eyes watering from the sting just beneath my eye. Fenrir's eyes snap open, the glow making him so otherworldly even to my own eyes.

Thump.

My body tenses, preparing to fight the Fae. If that look is anything to go by, he is ready for some blood, and I'm his target. My own energy blasts under my skin as it itches to be unleashed. I know Fenrir is much older and, by default, much stronger than me. I also know somewhere deep in my soul that I can take him and come out of this alive.

Daywalker or not, the Fae does not stand a chance in this fight.

"Enough!" Zoltan's voice brings everything snapping back to normal like a broken rubber band.

Jolted out of the trance-like state, I stumble back a step and look around in confusion. What the hell just happened? Fenrir is not murmuring anymore, yet everyone around us is still suspended in time and space.

"Thank you," Fenrir tells a pissed-off Zoltan, who is walking right at me like he wants to rip my head off. The Fae's face twists in a grimace, like it's too painful to show gratitude to the vampire.

"What were you thinking!" Snapping, Zoltan glares daggers at me, but I know his question is for Fenrir.

Argoz's bony fingers grip the sides of the broken wall, dragging his body through it like some creepy crawler. Without missing a step, Zoltan's hand lifts at the ghoul flicking his wrist. Argoz's human form appears, and he flops on his ass, leaning on the wall and breathing hard.

"How…" My words cut off when Zoltan stops, again too close for my liking, and his hand cups my face. His thumb glides over the cut under my eye, the feeling of my skin closing up and healing stunning me into silence.

"No!" Fenrir's protest is too late. "Don't taste her blood." The last part is dragged out slowly, as an afterthought.

Lifting his thumb, Zoltan pushes it between his lips, cleaning off my blood from it as the Fae finishes his sentence. His too-blue eyes flash for just a second with some inner power that rakes tremors in my body. Closing my eyes, I wish someone will just kill me and get it over with. If things keep going at this rate, I don't doubt that Fenrir's warning, that something worse than death coming for me, will come true.

"What were the two of you thinking?" Finally, Zoltan turns his attention away from me. I don't need to open my eyes to know it because I *physically* feel it every time he is looking at me.

"You should ask Argoz." Fenrir's words are sharp and choppy. "Threatening me in the middle of a hallway? I thought you had more brains than that. If not, go eat some. It'll do you good."

Ghouls feed on souls and bodies. Disgusting for sure, but it's not like they chose to be what they are. Just like me, they are stuck being what the fates decided. I've seen some of them, but fortunately, I haven't had too many encounters like this one before. The demon is nowhere to be found, but the ghoul kept coming. I'm not sure it would've been easy to get rid of Argoz if Zoltan didn't show up. Not that I'll ever admit that to the arrogant vampire.

"He already knew." My words are flat when I answer Fenrir's unspoken question. Zoltan was aware I'm a half blood long before tasting my blood from his fingers. The wariness in the glances he keeps sending my way is enough of a hint to what the Fae is thinking. "Don't ask me how."

The bow-shaped lips flatten in a thin white line of Fenrir's face, but he only gives me a sharp nod. Unwilling to dwell on it since there is nothing I can do to change it, I look around us at the frozen people again.

"How are you still doing this?" Watching Fenrir with suspicion, I see Zoltan turning his head my way from the corner of my eye. My whole body becomes alert at that.

"He is not." Zoltan's deep voice thrums through me.

"Zoltan teaches Mind Control and Physical Power Control," Argoz supplies in a shaky voice as he lifts himself off the floor. "That's how he forced me to change back… thank the fates."

"Of course, he does." My voice sounds just as flat as when the Fae told me his specialty. "I mean, why wouldn't I get all the weirdos here following me around like a bad smell I can't shake off? You couldn't possibly be a History or Science professor; I'm not lucky enough to be surrounded by nerds instead of brutes."

"I teach Supernatural History." Argoz offers a strained smile, his lips firmly pressed together. Maybe those razor teeth are not gone yet? A shiver makes me twitch.

"You and I are best buddies from now on, Argoz." To my embarrassment, my hand still trembles when I point the finger at him. "But no sharp teeth and trying to bite anymore, okay? I'm not that kinky with my friends."

All three of them laugh, albeit they all sound a little forced. Zoltan flicks his wrist again, assaulting my ears with the sudden noise of everyone coming back to life. They all look around confused, gaping at the massive hole in the wall across from where the four of us are standing. Fenrir must've noticed that I'm glued to the spot and unable to move because he walks up to me, grabbing my elbow again.

"Let us eat breakfast, shall we?" Fenrir leads me away.

My feet move woodenly along the hallway. Acid churns in my stomach at the mention of food, but I would rather be anywhere else than be stared at here. Two sets of eyes drill holes into the back of my head as Zoltan and Argoz follow behind us.

You'll be fine. Even my inner voice doesn't sound so sure anymore.

Chapter Fifteen

Walking through the open double doors in the dining area is like stepping into a different building. I expected a lot of tables with plain chairs around them and a long counter where you line up to grab food on a tray, all coming from my limited time in education at the only high school Sienna has. I'm very imaginative that way, my sarcasm bleeding into everything concerning the academy.

My lips part in awe of what I'm looking at.

Opposite the doors is a wall made entirely of floor-to-ceiling windows, allowing the silvery glow of the moon to reach inside and caress the fishbone parquet floor, as well as the long wooden tables set up with piles of food stretching out at the center of the area. Comfortable-looking couches and armchairs line the walls around us, and long coffee tables covered with the same platters piled high mountains of food mingle with the rest. It seems more like an extremely large family dinner than a dining hall for academy students. My stomach growls from the smell of baked meats and loaves of bread, saturating the air, and I'm not even hungry.

"I think we found one place that she likes." Fenrir's voice sounds amused, but I can't find enough motivation to look away from the relaxed atmosphere.

"Second place she likes," Zoltan chirps arrogantly. He is such a killjoy. "She had the same look on her face when I found her in the training hall."

I ignore them both.

"Miss Drake?" Clearing his throat, Argoz does get my attention as I'm led towards one of the empty seats. "I would like to apologize for my overreaction earlier." His eyes dart around my face, not locking gazes with me. "The aggression in the air triggered my response." Shoving his fingers in the collar of his shirt, he yanks on it as if it's choking him. "It's no excuse, and I'm not making one, I assure you. Having in mind my age, you would expect me to have more control. But you…" Shaking his head, he keeps pulling at the collar of the shirt, stretching it out to the point that the seams rip. "I've never felt anything like it. Nor have I seen anyone move or react that fast in the long centuries." Glancing subtly at the other two men, he finally meets my eyes. "Not even Zoltan."

My heart does a painful bump against my ribcage.

"Apology accepted." Seeing that we are standing around empty seating lining the wall, I plop in one of the armchairs so none of them can sit next to me. "It's not a safe world outside those gates of yours, Argoz." Choosing my words carefully, I pretend I don't see Fenrir and Zoltan still standing, as if daring each other who will move first and sit closest to me. "I have trained to protect myself, and no matter how hard I try, I can never control how I react in different situations. You could say I have a strong survival instinct. I don't think I react." There, that should satisfy his curiosity.

"Interesting." Oblivious to the tension of the other two, he moves to the couch, leaning over the hand rest, his face as close as he can get to me. I almost grin when Fenrir and Zoltan turn their glares on the ghoul. "As I said, I teach Supernatural History, yet I have never heard of a Fae with that speed. Which Court did you say you're from?"

"Seelie."

"Unseelie."

Both Zoltan and Fenrir speak at the same time. I can't help it. I roll my eyes so hard I think I pull a muscle. Argoz looks at all of us with a frown, his head tilted, surely debating if we all jumped on the crazy train.

"My mother is from the Seelie Court, my father from the Unseelie Court." Looking pointedly at the two idiots, I make sure they know I'm saving their assess, and they need to thank me later.

The historian in Argoz wins over the confusion and suspicion. He turns his full attention to me while the two men shuffle around, finding their own seats. Fenrir sits next to Argoz, and Zoltan plants his firm butt, not that I've been looking, in the armchair opposite mine. I wish he didn't. The strained smile, which I'm sure is making me look constipated, says as much.

Zoltan smirks.

I grind my teeth.

"That is a rare pairing to be sure." Argoz continues. The ghoul really is oblivious. "Usually, they all stick to their own."

"Yes, yes, they do." Deciding to irk the Fae, I smile brightly at Argoz. "But they realized that sticking to their own ends in offspring leaving things to be desired." I look pointedly at Fenrir, my smile growing when his nostrils flare. "So, they tried mixing things up, leading to a newer, better version of Fae. Like Fae two point O, let's say." Thank you, human television. I might not be able to mingle with humans, but I soak up their TV like a sponge every chance I get.

"Oh." Argoz jerks back like I've slapped him, glancing at the Fae next to him warily.

Zoltan laughs.

"Francesca fancies herself a great comedian, my friend." Fenrir moves closer to the edge of the couch, grabbing a plate and piling food on it while ignoring Zoltan's laugh and my proud grin. "But, let's not get sidetracked here. While we have time to talk, I would like to hear more about this second request. My mate's jokes or family tree can wait for later."

My smile drops, and the vampire cuts off his laughter abruptly. Two killjoys. Because one of them is not enough in a hundred-mile radius. Fenrir smiles politely at both of us before shifting his body so he is facing the ghoul better.

"Right." Argoz grabs the collar of his shirt again. I'm beginning to think that's his tic when he is nervous or uncomfortable. "They look identical, and I admit I was so taken aback that I didn't even think to check the signature."

"And you trusted a guard more than your own knowledge of my character." It's said conversationally, but there is no mistaking the accusation of those words.

If I didn't know that Fenrir did indeed trick the academy into bringing me here so I can snoop around, I would've accused the ghoul of being a shitty friend as well. But I am here, and I know better. Fenrir looks regal and arrogant as he sweeps his long hair away from his face, securing it in at the back of the head. It makes me wonder how many of the things he said to me are the truth and how many a manipulation.

No one said the Fae don't like to twist words to pursue their own agendas.

"You must understand that the tension has been running high from the moment she stepped foot in front of the gates." Giving me an apologetic glance, Argoz continues. "First, she ended up on our grounds without passing the trials, although after what I just saw, I can see how that is possible. Then came the attack right before the guard burst through my doors, telling me we approved two guests to enter. One of which is here causing havoc, and there is no sign of the other."

"Whoa, whoa, hang on there for a second. We will get back to Fenrir's hurt pride in a minute." My spine snaps straight at that information. "Let's get back to the part of the attack, huh? That horrible sound that brought me to my knees was an attack on the academy?"

All three of them press their mouths in a flat line, clamming up. Like hell they'll hide this from me now that the cat is out of the bag. I'll beat it out of them if I have to. Giving the vampire a fast once over, I amend my own declaration. I'll try my best to beat it out of them. The ghoul will be my best bet, followed by the Fae.

"Listen." Trying to reason with them, I soften my scowl. "At the moment, I'm here with you, and my life is on the line as well. I deserve to know if I'm in danger and what that danger is." Looking from one to the other, I linger on Argoz. "So, I can protect myself if I have to." Adding a few wide-eyed flutters of my eyelashes, I can see it's working when his face softens.

Zoltan and Fenrir both snort.

I ignore them as usual.

"You have nothing to worry about, Miss Drake. You are safe here." Argoz hurries to assure me. "The humans discovered one of the portals we use to exit and enter Sienna. The poor fools think they'll gain something if they pass through it, unaware the only thing awaiting them is death. It doesn't stop them from trying, though." He shakes his head like the humans are misbehaving children.

The air is lodged like a fist in my throat, and I find it difficult to breathe. What might be an annoyance to the Daywalkers can mean certain death, or maybe even a mass slaughter if humans do get past a portal. Most of the residents in Sienna have never seen a human, apart from on TV. They are like fictional characters to them. If they come face to face, the supernaturals will either get killed while standing in shock, or their instincts will take over and they'll tear the humans apart. We are stronger, yes, but the humans win in numbers. I doubt a handful of them can create something to bring a freak like me to her knees. The ghoul can downplay it as much as he likes, but this is huge, and Roberti needs to know about it like yesterday.

"They will not get through." Zoltan sounds so sure my eyes jerk to his face. I stare at him for so long that he repeats it again slowly. "They will *not* get through."

"You know this how?" Chewing on the inside of my mouth, I search his face. "They shouldn't have found the portal either."

"That's an entirely different problem," Fenrir speaks, the food forgotten on his plate. "We will deal with that as soon as we can."

"You have someone working with the humans." Realization slams me so hard it almost leaves me breathless. "You have one of your own working with them to bring us all down."

"There have always been those that get too ambitious and try to bring this institution down, Francesca." Fenrir squares his shoulders. "All of them learn the error of their ways sooner than they expect. You can be sure this will end soon, too."

"Do you already have an idea who's behind it?" Something nudges at the back of my mind, but I can't quite grasp it.

"Not yet." Nostrils flaring, he looks pained to admit it. His eyes glow for a second, getting my attention.

"The guards!" My shout is much louder than I expected, and I slap a hand over my mouth.

"What are you talking about, that's impossible…" Argoz gets defensive instantly.

"Let her speak." Zoltan shuts him up mid-sentence. "What about the guards?"

My mind goes back to the moment when I met the demon, but the words are stuck in my throat. Flicking my eyes at the ghoul, I swallow thickly, unsure if I should just shut my mouth and wait until I can inform Roberti. I'm sure the agency has a stake in this too. Fenrir sees my indecision and, reaching over Argoz, grabs hold of my clammy hand.

"You can say whatever it is in front of both of them." He squeezes my fingers reassuringly. "None of them are involved in anything that will harm the residents of Sienna. You have my word."

"When I first saw the demon that was with you"— Jerking my chin towards Argoz, I wrap my fingers around Fenrir's simply to ground myself, so I can think— "he was talking to someone about the portal and me coming to visit the academy." All three of them stare at me intently as I rack my brain to remember what they said exactly. "They mentioned something about taking a stand and not wanting the meddling vampire to stick his nose in their business. I'm guessing that's you and your winning personality, Zoltan."

He grunts, and my joke falls flat.

"Anyway…" Blowing a breath through pursed lips, I roll my shoulders, releasing Fenrir's hand, much to his displeasure. "They were talking about having plans about the portal, keeping the two of you away from it and also looking into why Fenrir wanted me here. Whoever the other person was that the demon was talking to knows you were outside the academy. They thought you helped me pass the trials."

The three of them exchange a look that pisses me off instantly.

"Come now, children, let's share with the class, shall we?" Glaring at all of them, I folded my arms across my chest. "I told you what I heard, so you can extend the same courtesy."

"The guards are either demons, shifters, or mages," Argoz says in such a way you'd think he is telling a story. "We can't know who the guard spoke to unless we know where his rooms are. They are each separated by species."

"He was in the hallway to the left of where Fenrir's rooms are." My eyebrows hit my hairline. "The two of you live with the guards?" Looking from the vampire to the Fae, I can't help the glee in my expression.

"We took rooms there when this mess started, so we can keep an eye on things. Easier for the guards to get hold of us that way." Sniffing, Fenrir looks down his nose at me. "We do not live there."

"Excuse me for the insult of thinking you are like the rest of us, your majesty." I expected the ghoul and the vampire to laugh.

They don't.

"You are forgiven," Fenrir tells me primly, and I get my tenth shock in twenty-four hours.

"You are from the Royal Court?" I realized my mistake as soon as the words left my mouth.

"She's supposed to be your mate!" Argoz jumps so suddenly that I jump to my feet along with him.

"He's been hiding his royal bloodline, testing me if I'm only after his status." Another lie spoken instantly. It makes me doubt if I'll ever be able to tell the truth.

"We need to speak to the guards," Zoltan states, the two of them standing as well, the cold food left untouched on the table. I guess we all lost our appetites.

"I'm coming with you." When he opens his mouth to argue, I cut him off. "Those assholes owe me a bike. And I need the bag of clothes that I'm sure didn't survive."

Chapter Sixteen

Burying my face in the soft pillow, I breathe in the fresh scent of something subtle and floral. Detergent is my guess. Stretching my arms over my head, I point my toes straight under the covers, groaning when my muscles protest. The conversations Zoltan and Fenrir were having with the guards proved to be boring as hell, and I was falling asleep on my feet. They convinced me to go rest only after they both gave their solemn oaths to tell me everything they learn in my absence. I even won the argument of having my own room instead of sharing Fenrir's, and most of my words were incoherent and mumbled. A smile stretches on my face. Those two have no idea who they are dealing with. I can drive the unfeasible Roberti insane when I'm trying very hard not to, so the two of them don't stand a chance.

It's a natural talent of mine.

Too soon, my mind clears the fog of sleep and starts to process everything. Wincing when I fling the covers away, I grind my teeth so I can get off the bed. Bypassing their damn trials—or so they keep telling me, although I'm not convinced—was more workout than I've gotten in years. Add to that bleeding from my ears, and soon after fighting a demon and a ghoul, a girl needs a break.

Or to get laid, my internal nympho supplies helpfully, adding flashes of Zoltan's face and body as an added motivation to get things her way.

"Whatever." Muttering under my breath, I scoop up the pants and a shirt Fenrir was kind enough to find for me. Apparently, I intimidate the students in my leathers stained in blood. "And whose fault is that? Their crazy asses require you to die so you can come here. Idiots!" Riling myself up, cursing up a storm, I head for the shower.

It's too soon when the water starts turning cold while I'm letting the spray pelt my neck and shoulders. Leaving my head to hang to my chest, I endure it as long as I can. When goosebumps start popping up on my arms, I wash my hair hastily, yanking on it hard, bringing forward another current of curses echoing in the bathroom. The longer I think about everything, the more worked up I get.

Knowing full well I'll only get into trouble if I keep stewing in anger, I dress as quickly as I can before rushing out of the room like the hounds of Hell are on my heels. Slowing down only when I find my way back to the weapons room that Zoltan called the training hall, I take a deep breath and walk through the door.

No one is here.

It's either too early, or too late, but I don't care. I'm not looking to mingle with anyone. It's perfect for doing my yoga stretches that Roberti scoffs and laughs about. The brute thinks unless you have bruises or blood dripping from you, nothing else is considered a workout. He changed his mind when the flexibility I got from it made it difficult for him to hold onto me when we were sparring. Grinning at the memory, I yank the shirt over my head, leaving me in my sports bra. It's a good thing I wear those. No one needs the girls bouncing around when you are trying not to get killed. Which happens to me often.

Too often, if I'm honest.

Concentrating on my breathing, I block out everything else. My body moves in sync with the air, going in and out of my lips. With my eyes closed, I allow my limbs to flow like water, twisting and turning with each breath. Too soon, I feel someone's energy probing mine, their nearness alerting my senses. Since I don't recognize it, I keep my eyes closed, ignoring their presence.

Quite unfortunate that they don't ignore mine.

"Is that some secret Fae killing technique?" A female voice snickers, followed by another giggle and a male snort.

Bending one knee and with my back leg straight, I spread my arms wide, keeping the warrior pose. I like this pose.

"Maybe it's a Fae dance technique." Another female voice chirps, nasally and high pitched.

My torso turns, my shoulders lining up with my bent knee as I lift my arms over my head, fingers pointed at the ceiling. Breathe in. Hold, Breathe out.

"It does look like a stupid dance," the first female adds. "Maybe she is deaf. I heard her ears were bleeding last night."

My skin prickles when one of them walks too close. Stiffening, I expect whoever it is to do something, but they just stand there. Deciding to end this, I bring both arms down at the same time as my feet touch together. Keeping my breathing even, I try to ground myself, imagining roots growing from the soles of my feet into the floor. I've never been good at this part. It doesn't stop me from trying. I'm nothing if not determined.

The air gets disturbed around my face, and I'm wishing these imaginary roots were real so I can yank one out and stab whoever is waving a hand in front of me in the eye. Grinding my teeth, I try to ignore it. The air ruffles the hairs that have dried out and escaped my braid. My hand shoots out, snatching the arm of the asshole standing too close for my liking, and I twist it behind their back. A shrill, high-pitched scream tells me it's one of the girls even before I open my eyes.

"It's rude to interrupt people while they are trying to concentrate." Pushing her arm up higher between her shoulder blades, I grin at the other two that are gaping at me like they've seen a ghost. "You look like you're my age." Glancing at the kneeling woman, I smile at her glare. "Acting like a child."

Her chocolate brown hair is pulled tight in a high pony-tail, opening her beautiful face up. Too bad it's made ugly by the scrunched-up nose and sneer on her lips. If she thinks I'll get scared by the grimace, the girl needs to work more on her facial expressions.

"Let her go, you nut job!" the redhead still standing next to a beefy, dark-haired guy shrieks.

"You are poking at me while I'm trying to find my center, and I'm the nut job?" Snorting, I push the idiot away and straighten. "How does that work?"

"You're trying to find what?" The redhead looks confused for a second. Her nasally voice grinds on my nerves. "You know what? Never mind! Apologize at once!"

Scratching my ear, I watch her face for a second. Yup, she's actually serious with the nonsense that came out of her mouth. Shaking my head, I snatch the shirt off the floor, pulling it over my head. So much for calming down my anger.

"I think she has selective hearing." The beefy guy grumbles from next to the redhead.

"What are you? Her psychologist?" The brown eyed glare is turned in his direction. "Go hang out with her then." Lifting her chin up, the redhead looks down her nose at me. Impressive since she is a head shorter. "I said apologize." The brunette even crosses her arms, watching me expectantly.

Heading straight between the two of them, they both flinch when I reach them. With a smirk, I bump my shoulder into the redhead, making her stumble. Something between a gasp and a shout comes out of her, and my grin stretches as I head for the door.

"I'll think about it."

I don't reach the door.

Sharp nails dig into my shoulder, ripping the only clean shirt I have. My body reacts to the aggression like always as I pivot to face the redhead. My hand shoots out, the heel of my palm connecting with her jaw. Her head snaps back, and I follow it with two fast punches in her sternum. She drops like a rock and curls in on herself. My knees bend, preparing my body to pounce on her and end this right here, right now.

"Francesca, stop!" Fenrir's voice snaps me out of my killing daze.

When my mind is clear enough, I see the other two idiots watching me in horror, their wide eyes going from me to their writhing friend on the floor. Fenrir steps next to me, his fingers wrapping like a vice around my elbow. The Fae sure loves his elbow holding.

"I'm fine." Jerking my arm, I try to dislodge him, but he

holds on like a leech. Grinding my teeth, I turn to him. "I said I'm fine. And stop calling me Francesca; you're not my mother."

"That is your name. What shall I call you if not by your name?" He looks genuinely perplexed.

"Whatever you want, as long as it isn't my full name spoken like I'm a child throwing a tantrum."

"Okay." Dragging the words out, a line forms between his eyebrows. I stare at him with a slacked jaw. He is actually thinking about it right now. "Hellion."

"Excuse me?"

"Hellion." The Fae actually grins at me. "I can't think of a better name for you, Francesca Drake."

"Sir, this female…" The brunette opens her mouth, but Fenrir waves her away like a pesky fly.

"I'm well aware of your antics around the academy. This should teach you to pick your opponents more wisely in the future. If you cannot deal with a few bruises and a hurt ego, you do not belong here. Now get out of my face, all of you."

When they spring into action scurrying like cockroaches, lifting their friend and dragging her along, I don't miss the poisonous looks sent my way. Staying quiet, I watch them leave, waiting until I can no longer feel their energy nearby. Then I round on Fenrir.

"Great job." Jamming my hands on my hips, I'm surprised when he takes a step back. "Like I needed more enemies watching my every step around this place. Why are you even here?"

"Looking for you." Catching himself, he moves closer to me. "You need an escort, remember?"

"How can I ever forget, your majesty." Turning on my heel, I almost jog away from him.

"You are still upset about me not telling you." His long legs make it easy for him to fall into step with me.

"You think?"

"But you knew before you got here because I told you at the bar, Hellion." I might break a tooth because of this guy. My jaw clenches so tight, I hear my teeth grinding.

"That's a lie." It sounds like a growl when I push the words out.

"I told you that you are one of mine." He almost bumps into me when I stop abruptly.

Giving him a once over, lingering on his light eyes and platinum hair, my eyebrows lift up on my forehead. "I have absolutely no connection to the Light Court, Fenrir."

"I'm Unseelie." Grinning proudly, he puffs up his chest.

"But…" My words die out when the blue color of his eyes swirls and red eyes with white pupils are staring back at me, unblinking.

"Phantasmagoria, remember?"

"Illusion…" My hand lifts to his face, the tips of my fingers touching the corner of his eye.

"Yes." His voice sounds deeper, huskier, and I snatch my hand back.

"Okay, then." Feeling awkward, I think of anything to change the subject. "Did you find out anything useful after I left?"

"You didn't leave. I carried your half-asleep body to the separate rooms that you demanded."

"As I said"—Ignoring his comment, I get moving again — "after I left." Shoving a hand in his face to shut him up when he opens his mouth again, I don't turn my head to look at him. I'm still unnerved by the illusion crap. "Did you hear anything useful?"

The Fae looks like he wants to push his point, but he

luckily decides against it. "We have no names, but some of the guards have noticed discrepancies in the ranks. We have a few of our trusted ones keeping an ear out. We will find them, Hellion. It's just a matter of time."

"Time, we don't have, Fenrir." Forgetting the discomfort, I turn to look at his face. "The Daywalkers might be able to deal with this since you are better equipped. The residents of Sienna that are disappearing and showing up dead can't. They count on Roberti...on me to keep them safe." Now that I've had some sleep and my brain is not fried, I remember other things too.

A shiver like ghostly fingers runs up my spine.

"I need to tell you what happened before you saw me first at Raven's Feather." Chewing on the inside of my mouth, I try to think of how to say it without sounding like I have mental problems.

"Zoltan is meeting us at the dining hall. Let's hold the conversation until we get there. Even the walls have ears, and it's difficult to block the sound while I'm moving."

"You can actually do that?"

"I can do many things." Giving me a strained smile, if I'm not mistaken, Fenrir looks embarrassed.

Well, I'll be damned. The arrogant jerk is shy.

Filing that revelation away for a later time, I keep my mouth shut and follow him to the dining hall. The fluttering in my belly and the speeding up of my heartbeat have absolutely nothing to do with the frustratingly annoying vampire we are about to meet.

Nope.

It's just my nerves because I need to tell them about the shadows from that night. *Keep lying to yourself.* My snarky inner voice laughs at the pathetic attempt to delude myself.

Chapter Seventeen

My head swivels left and right as we walk the halls of the academy. With everything pressing on me from all sides, most of all my inadequacy to have control of my crazy genes, I forget that standing here is every supernatural creature's dream. I, too, dreamed that one day I would be here, learning how to walk the daylight and the human realm. A dream that was squished like a bug under a shoe by my ever-realistic mother. As I watch the people around me pass us by, all of them hurrying to a place they need to be, I hear her voice as if she's standing next to me.

"You are half blood, Francesca. Those like you hardly live long enough to reach maturity, much less dream of becoming a Daywalker. You will do best to stay as far away from that place as you can. Daywalkers don't tolerate half-bloods. And without them, our world will fall apart. You don't want to be the downfall for the rest of us. Learn your place, girl, while you still have time."

Fear tightens my chest, my palms dampening with cold sweat.

What was wrong with me that I actually thought that this was a good idea? I should've said no. Damn, I should've told Roberti screw you and then walked away from everything.

Glancing sideways at Fenrir, I hope he doesn't notice when I wipe my hands on my pants, swallowing the lump that is like a fist in my throat. This is why I do stupid things and get myself in trouble. If I stop for long enough and start thinking, anxiety and damnation of what I am will crush me. The weight of my doomed existence will either drive me insane or I'll end it all on my own.

I'm prickly instead.

The mask I dawn and carry with pride has kept everything and everyone away from me. If you don't let anyone close, they can't see your vulnerability. They'll never learn your secrets.

Like you didn't let Zoltan learn your vulnerability? The inner voice never seizes to remind me of my shortcomings.

"What are you thinking?" My heart stutters at Fenrir's voice.

"Nothing." When he turns those searching eyes my way, I find the walls and windows around us fascinating. "Well, nothing important. Just wondering about this place. It's not every day I get to walk with the rest of your kind."

"It's my kind now, is it?" The light of the moon through the large windows catches his iris, a flash of something startling me for a split second. When I blink, it's gone, and that's enough to convince me I imagined it.

"You are a Daywalker, are you not Fae?"

"Ah." Nodding as if he expected as much, his gaze narrows slightly as he folds his hands at his lower back. "That I am." He dips his chin in greeting to a few students that watch him starry eyed.

"You don't sound very happy about it." Concentrating

not to fidget with my hands, my nostrils flare, catching the scent of many species nearby.

"Happy?" One of his perfect eyebrows climbs up his forehead. "I'm neither happy nor unhappy, Hellion. I am what I am." His gaze sweeps over me from head to toe, sending an awareness prickling under my skin. "Just like you are what you are."

"We both know that's not true." Mumbling under my breath, I flick my eyes around, making sure no one is close enough to hear us. "You are what every one of us wishes to become, and very few achieve it. Which reminds me…" Against my better judgment, I move closer to him, wrapping my fingers around his forearm. "Why is it that very few graduate this academy? What exactly are the rest of you doing to all the people willing to risk their lives to train and join you."

"You will do well to leave things alone, Francesca." When he says my name, his voice is flat and devoid of emotion. "I helped you get in so we can stop the insanity that might be the end of all of us, not for you to poke around in what does not concern you. Heed my advice and leave things alone. Find what you are looking for, then leave."

Many things sit on the tip of my tongue, but the urge to point out to him where to stick his advice is the strongest of them all. The way his body shifts to the side away from me, the muscles under the fabric of his shirt that I'm gripping turning to granite, warns me to stay silent. I don't think the Fae is aware of the little tells he subconsciously gives me to drop the subject. Or maybe he is and did it on purpose. Fenrir is just another mystery in this place that is making me itch to discover its secrets. The feeling of being watched presses like a finger between my shoulder blades, making me agree with the Fae that I should care less about the academy and more about finding the archives before getting the hell out of here.

My feet falter, slowing down when we reach the same split hallway, one leading to the dining hall and the other adorned in golden tones and accents. The pull is much stronger this time, and the effort to resist it has beads of sweat forming around my hairline. Fenrir's hand covers mine where my fingers are digging into the shirt on his forearm, bringing me to the present. When I look at his face, his profile is as stern as always, his gaze trained straight in front of us, unaware that he has stopped me from bolting down that hall, no doubt saving me from a guaranteed death. Whatever is there can't be anything good. Not if everyone ignores it, and it calls to me like a siren song.

No, that is a damn trap if I've ever seen one.

"You should smile." Still keeping his eyes straight, Fenrir pets my fingers a few times before dropping his hand away. "You look like you'll either kill someone, or I'm the worst company a female can have."

"I don't get your point." Deadpanning it, I deepen my glower.

Throwing his head back, the bursts of his deep belly laughter startles the few people mulling the hallway. My lips quirk at the corners, but I manage to keep a straight face. He might not be a bad guy, but it doesn't mean that he is not hiding something. I need to stop acting like a fool and get moving. The longer I stay here, the chances are we are all going to regret this little adventure. Everything so far points to that. Too many coincidences are never a good thing.

I feel the weight of Zoltan's gaze the second my feet cross the dining room threshold. Those deep blue eyes settle on my hand, still gripping Fenrir's forearm. I drop it like he burnt me, not missing the displeased groan coming from the Fae's chest. Another thing telling me I should get out of here as fast as my feet will carry me.

The constant hum of conversation filling the air calms my unease, while my feet keep moving in the direction of the side table where Zoltan is sitting alone. The plates are full of food, spread in front of him untouched, as he tracks my movement like a predator marking his prey. All my nerve endings come to life, the urge to flee so intense I almost turn around and bolt out of the room. Clenching my fists, I grind my teeth, fighting the instinct with everything in me.

Zoltan's full lips curve slightly at the corners.

Seeing that smirk prickles my pride, shaking off whatever idiocy he provoked in me. I shouldn't have let him see my reaction to him, but it's too late now. I've shown more of my weaknesses to this man than anyone else in my life. It needs to stop, and it needs to stop now.

"Let's sit with him since no one likes his company or sunny personality." Waving my hand in Zoltan's direction, I grin at Fenrir. "I've always had a soft spot for the unfortunate ones."

The room falls so silent you can hear a pin drop. Fenrir chokes on air, his face reddening while he hacks like a cat trying to cough out a hairball. Anxiety tries to push its way through me, but I wrestle it down, keeping the grin plastered on my face. Locking my gaze on Zoltan's, I regret opening my mouth so much, I'm grateful I don't start apologizing immediately. His smoldering gaze burns me all the way to my soul.

And then he chuckles.

"Miss Drake, a pleasure to see you, as always." I hate

that my eyes trace the shaking of his chest while he still chuckles.

"Because you've seen me what?" Plopping across from him, I lift my eyebrow, "Twice now?"

My heart does a hard and painful thump against my ribs at the look crossing his eyes. It's gone so fast it leaves my head spinning, but I will bet everything I am that it was there. Fenrir rounds the table opposite me, bumping his leg on Zoltan's knee. The gesture is too obvious to go unnoticed. Has Zoltan seen me before? If so, when was that? My stomach drops to the floor at the weird exchange, but I have no time to think it through. Not right now, at least.

"She came across Cassius's daughter and her minions when I found her." Fenrir speaks conversationally, jerking his pants up at the knees as he sits down all prim and proper.

"You do know that I'm not a stray dog that you adopted, right?" Glaring at Fenrir, I ignore the penetrating gaze that Zoltan hasn't moved away from me.

"Don't be absurd, Francesca. He should be aware that we might have a problem, thanks to your little adventure this morning." The arrogant Fae is back to looking down his nose at me. I didn't even notice when he slipped the mask on.

"I was trying to find my center." Refusing to apologize for not doing anything wrong, I stare the Fae down. He is trying very hard not to laugh, which only deepens my glare. "She touched me, which made her fair game after that. Who touches anyone without permission?"

"I do." Zoltan's deep voice makes me shiver for an entirely inappropriate reason.

"It speaks!" Blurting out the words a lot louder than I intended, I make Fenrir almost swallow his tongue. "Sorry."

Squeezing my eyes shut as if pained, I pray for the ground to open so I can disappear.

A sound like large rocks rolling down a steep hill snaps my eyes open. Slowly but surely, it gets louder and louder, the only noise in the otherwise silent space. My shocked gaze stays on Zoltan, who hasn't moved a muscle or looked away from me since I walked in this dining hall. The only difference at the moment is the empty look in his deep, blue eyes.

"I believe you have found your match, Zoltan." A voice like grinding rocks speaks, surging panic through my veins.

Zoltan stiffens.

"Cassius, I didn't know you were back." Fenrir luckily is capable of speech. I watch him stand up, reaching his arm to shake someone's hand.

A shadow falls over the table announcing the person so close to us now that I can feel my skin prickling by his nearness. Neither Zoltan nor I break eye contact, but he gives me nothing. No indication if this person being here is a good or a bad thing. And then the name penetrates my panicked thoughts. With a groan, I look up to tell him he can ask his daughter to settle her own problems.

The words die on my tongue.

Chapter Eighteen

A mountain of a man looms over the table. His body is relaxed, but danger screams at me while he handles my perusal with a smile on his roguish face. His jaw is too square, and his eyes are set too wide apart to be beautiful, but the harshness of his features, and the leather patch with a golden symbol covering his left eye, gives him an irresistible appeal. His muscles have muscles, and his legs look like tree trunks from this close. Dark auburn hair is cut short at the sides, the longer strands at the top combed neatly away from his forehead. Unlike everyone else I've seen so far, he is dressed in a tailored suit, no doubt made custom for him. The color matches with the dress code here, which is obviously black with gold, the thin golden tie lying flat on his broad chest confirming my assumptions. The one eye that is watching me with curiosity is so light brown, it's almost yellow.

"I was told your guest has arrived." Cassius turns away from me, and I take a deep breath, realizing I wasn't breathing while we stared at each other.

"Yes." Fenrir squares his shoulders, preening. "This is Francesca Drake." The Fae shoves his hand in my face as if expecting me to take it. I stare at it like it's a snake that will bite me. "My mate." The last two words jolt me out of the insanity, and I snatch Fenrir's fingers with a punishing grip and climb to my feet.

"Very pleased to meet you." Knowing full well that only a blind person will miss the paling of my face, I flutter my lashes at Cassius. His smile slips, and a line forms between the harsh slash of his eyebrows when I stab a hand at his chest for a handshake.

"She acts weird when she is nervous." Zoltan rubs a hand over his face like he can't stand seeing me embarrass myself.

"I see." Cassius takes my outstretched hand, his plate-sized palm engulfing my fingers like a steel trap. I fight the instinct screeching inside me to snatch it back. "My daughter said she is aggressive, so I must say I expected something else."

"You shouldn't touch people without permission." My mouth keeps talking despite my need to stay quiet. Or run away.

"And why is that, little Fae?" That one almost yellow eye stops my heart with its intensity.

That's when the most crucial thing hits me like a meteor on top of my head.

I feel nothing.

I'm touching his hand, skin on skin, and I feel no emotions, no energy, not a damn thing coming from him. He is very much alive, staring at me with a knowing look in his one eye as whatever blood I have running through me drains from my face. Only Fenrir is supposed to know who I am. That was the only reason Roberti convinced me to come here in the first place. First Zoltan, and now this guy —whoever he is—know, and that does not bode well for me. The longer I stare at Cassius, the surer I am that me being here has very little to do with the people in Sienna.

My heart slows down.

Thump.

"Oh shit! She's going to bolt." Fenrir's panicked hiss jerks me out of the trancelike state.

Stumbling back a step, I yank my hand out of Cassius's grasp, almost toppling over the armchair I was occupying a few moments ago. "Who are you people?" My eyes dart around looking for escape, anger burning in my chest because everyone else is totally ignoring our little group at the edge of the room. "What do you want from me?"

"Drake, calm down, let's not bring attention here. Sit so we can talk." Fenrir is trying to calm me down but only manages to irk me more.

"She has been here for two days." Cassius glares at the Fae. "Have you not spoken to her?"

Inching around the chair, I eye the open doors of the dining hall. If they keep their attention on each other, I can reach the hallway in time to have a head start. It might not be easy to get through the forest with all the boobytraps they have set up, but I passed through it with just a handful of bruises. I'm confident when running for my life that I'll get outside those gates with just a few scratches. Roberti will hide me after that, I have no doubt in my mind. I only need to get the hell out of this building.

"Franky, sit." Zoltan's soft words jerk my head in his direction. Hearing my nickname from his lips is enough to stop me dead in my tracks. "I will not allow anyone to hurt you."

Those are the same words he whispered to me while he

134

was holding me wrapped in his arms. A feeling of safety spreads through my limbs, making my legs shake and my fingers tremble. Three sets of eyes are trained on me, and I grab the back of the armchair to stay standing.

"Whose bright idea was it to meet here?" Fenrir turns a glare on Zoltan.

"You think that she would've come willingly to one of our rooms?" Zoltan speaks calmly like we are discussing something random, not my life. "Or that you could've stopped her when she decided to run?" His deep blue gaze searches mine. "We mean you no harm. All I ask is that you hear us out. You'll be free to go after that."

"You have lost your mind, Zoltan!" Cassius booms, and I jump away from them, my knees bending slightly.

Zoltan doesn't blink an eye, keeping his gaze on me. "Just hear what we have to say. You have nothing to lose at this point."

"Nothing but my life." Stabbing a finger at the vampire, something about the way he looked at it made the whole situation hilarious.

A burst of hysterical laughter bubbles up in my chest. Biting my lips, I try to contain it, but I have no such luck. A snort is followed by another until I'm leaning heavily on the back of the armchair, tears streaming down my face. Every time I lift my head, I see their wary faces watching me with concern, and the fit starts again.

I did have a feeling my life will end here; I just didn't know that it will be for nothing…that it would be a trap rather than protecting innocents.

Another thought strikes me, stopping all the laughter and giggles.

"Did you kidnap and then kill all those people just to trap me here?" Flicking my attention from face to face, I watch all their eyes widen at my accusation. "Wasn't there an easier way to trick me? Did you have to kill all of them for this?"

"How dare you accuse us..." Cassius snarls at me.

Zoltan moves so fast I'm startled when one second, he is sitting as if glued to the stupid chair, and in the next his broad back is obscuring my vision. Even now, with my life hanging by a thread, I can't help myself as I trace his broad shoulders and narrow waist with my eyes. The black pants stretching over his round, firm buttocks as he leans slightly forward seem to mold to him as he gets in Cassius's face.

"Back away from her now." Goosebumps prickle my arms at the soft words. "I don't wish to fight you, but I will. Fenrir will not be able to cover that up."

Remembering the Fae's words, that he can block everyone from hearing our conversation if he doesn't have to move, I inch to the side, glancing at the rest of the people in the dining hall. Most of them ignore us, with a dozen throwing concerned looks our way and a few staring bluntly in our direction. I'm guessing the three men facing off with each other will get attention even if they can't hear a word we say.

"You couldn't hide us from view?" I watch Fenrir's face like a hawk. If a muscle twitches the wrong way, I'll know he is lying.

"Everyone saw us come in, and they saw Zoltan sit here before we joined him. It's less of a problem to hide a conversation than it is to cast a full illusion." Shrugging unapologetically, the Fae lifts his chin up.

Those words calm me down more than any other words he might say. If they want me dead, I'm sure they won't go to those lengths. Fenrir could cast an illusion and let Zoltan kill me when the demon attacked, and Argoz lost his shit, shifting into his ghoul form. A shiver races up and down my spine, the gravity of the danger I am in settling in the marrow of my bones. They haven't killed me yet, because they need something from me. If I play my cards right, I might be able to get the hell out of here, but not if they watch my every move.

"I'll hear what you have to say." Without thinking, I place my hand right at the center of Zoltan's back.

He stiffens, muscles jumping under my palm.

Feeling stupid, berating myself for doing things without thinking, I start pulling it back when he leans more into my touch. My fingers spasm slightly, the need to move and trace his back almost bringing me to my knees. The next second he is gone, my palm caressing the air where he used to be. The other two didn't notice a thing, but that small shift in weight, a seemingly insignificant gesture, spoke volumes. It told me more than if Zoltan spent days trying to convince me he means no harm. It is an involuntary reaction, and the way he is avoiding my searching gaze right now confirms it. The vampire might not want me dead, but he still wants something.

I can work with that.

Ignoring the idiotic feeling telling me I'm being too harsh on Zoltan, I round the armchair and sit gingerly on the edge of the thick cushion. Looking pointedly at Fenrir and Cassius, I wait until they take their seats as well. When they keep glancing at each other, the blood boils in my veins, having just about enough of their crap.

"You needed me to hear you out. Let's go. If you speak fast enough, I might catch the bar open in Sienna. I need a drink or two after this." Folding my arms over my chest, I hide my still-trembling hands.

"You said you remembered something that you wanted

to share with me," Fenrir starts, but stops with a frown, my head already shaking before he is finished.

"Let me clarify how it's going to work, Fae." Glaring at him, my nails dig deeper into my skin to keep me grounded. "This will not be an exchange of information, so get that through your thick skull so we can move along. This is the part where you speak your peace, and if I don't like one word coming out of your mouth, I'm out of here so fast you'll think you imagined my presence."

"She is perfect." Cassius is looking at me with so much enthusiasm I want to puke.

"You must be special." My eyebrows climb up my forehead as I watch him with pity. "Half of your brain leaked the day you poked your eye out, didn't it?"

"That was uncalled for." The mammoth of a man sounds insulted, but he can't entirely hide the smile stretching his lips.

"None of these people you've seen here will pass the final exam to become a Daywalker." Zoltan, always the man of few words, says the words so matter a fact it is almost like he slapped me. "They are all going to die."

My eyes snap to his.

"You are killing them here?" Bile rises in the back of my throat, the acid burning my insides. "You trick them into risking their lives just so you can murder them here?"

"None of us are killing them, Francesca." Fenrir sounds wary, the words pushed out with difficulty as his eyes take on a troubled look. "In the last few decades, no one has passed the final exam. At first, we thought that those who passed the trial to join us here were not strong enough, despite the ancient magic allowing them passage."

"There aren't traps set up through the forest?" A tremor rakes my spine. The memory of the ancient magic that I felt chases away the foreboding feeling. It didn't feel wrong to me. Actually, it felt calming and inviting. *Like a spider trying to catch a fly.* The thought sours my mood.

"No, it's ancient magic trials set up from the day the academy was built. We haven't figured out where it feeds from, yet. Something is fueling it, but the source is a mystery to us."

"I still don't get what you're trying to tell me." My knee starts bouncing as I look from one to the next, all three men appearing determined. "What does any of this have to do with me?"

"From the beginning, we had four to nine graduates joining our ranks per generation." Cassius's rumbling voice vibrates in my belly. "The numbers started going down without raising red flags. Some generations are bred stronger than others." At my accusing glare, he simply shrugs. "It's a fact that cannot be disputed. Genetics work in strange ways. Anyway, no one thought it strange until it became one to three graduates per generation. The humans started poking our gateways, ambushing our teams, and forcing us to pay closer attention. When there was none in the last few decades, we started investigating."

Cassius sends a side look to Zoltan, but the vampire clenches his jaw so hard muscle spasms on one side. My knee bounces harder, anxiety making me jittery as hell. Why can't they just say whatever it is? All this storytelling is driving me nuts.

"And?" Prompting him when he stays quiet for too long, I want to scratch his eyes out when he gives me a displeased look.

"We came to the conclusion that whatever they are looking for, they haven't found it in the students attending the academy…"

"In the last few decades." I finish the sentence for him, my voice devoid of emotion.

"Yes." Cassius is searching my face, and I realize he expects me to put it together.

My mind is spinning with what they've told me so far. Ignoring Zoltan's intense eyes, I squeeze mine shut, blocking out all distractions. Everything I know so far—all that they've told me here in the last two days and what I heard from Roberti—floats like puzzle pieces switching and rearranging behind my closed eyelids.

My eyes snap open.

"They couldn't find it in the students passing the trials, so now they started searching through Sienna." Numbness covers me from head to toe, my bouncing knee stopping the erratic movement. "They are kidnaping people until they find whatever it is."

Daren's words come to mind. "Rumor has it, all of them were not as pure-blooded as we all believed."

"They are searching for half-bloods." Blurting it out makes it more real. "They need something only a half blood has."

"That's what we came down to, yes." Cassius nods slowly, watching me warily.

"Who are *they* exactly?" My lungs burn as I hold my breath and pray the first thing that comes to my mind is wrong.

I hate the fact that the one time I'm right about something, it signs my death warrant.

"The Board of the academy." Zoltan slams the nail in my coffin.

Chapter Nineteen

"The three of you are fucking insane!" Jumping off the armchair, I don't care anymore if I can't fight all three to get out of here.

At least I'll still have a chance.

"Sit down and hear us out." Cassius glares, bloating up like a pufferfish.

"You are out of your mind if you think I'm going to just sit here and wait for them to kill me. I'll die anyway, but at least I'll go swinging," Returning his glare, I let my fangs drop. "At your head."

Zoltan materializes in front of me, his fingers wrapping around my shoulders in a tight grip. Calmness blankets me, my body sagging in his hold. I have no idea why I get so riled up when they are trying to explain things to me. I know I should sit down and hear the rest of their plans before jumping to conclusions. Grateful for his reassurance, I lift my gaze, locking it with Zoltan's so I can thank him. The heat in his smoldering gaze lifts the fog from my mind.

Rage surges through me when I understand how he

always calms me down. The jerk is a master in mind control, and he thinks that's some smart shit to pull on me right now. Still watching him without blinking, my knee jerks up with as much strength as I can gather. Satisfaction is the greatest gift of them all when they find their target.

Zoltan doubles over, his hands dropping from my shoulders so they can wrap around his hopefully bruised balls. That should teach the arrogant fuck to mess with my brain. I don't get the pleasure to hear his pained scream, but I'm happy with the long, low groan reaching my ears. The other two suck in sharp breaths, and their eyes are about to pop out of their skulls. For Cassius's sake I hope he keeps his one eye.

So I can pull it out of his head in a minute.

"Don't you ever mess with my head, vamp." Leaning closer to Zoltan's ear, I suppress the shudder passing through me from his scent. "Next time, I will rip off your cock and feed it to you."

"I think she'll do it, too." Fenrir's voice sounds morbidly fascinated and terrified at the same time.

Zoltan chuckles, although it's a pain-filled sound.

"I deserved that." Straightening up, he winces while adjusting himself, and my treacherous eyes lock on his hand like Velcro. "Let's not try it again. Even my steel control has limits." I'm envious of my knee, which is plain stupid, and that's the reason I'm taken aback when I lift my gaze to his face.

His eyes are glowing brighter, the same blue color as they always are. Tiny veins branch out from his pupils, making them look like small suns spinning in the middle of his irises. I'm so fascinated by it that my upper body leans towards him so I can get a closer look. The only thing I succeed in doing is pressing my chest to his and bringing his mouth so near I can feel his breath fanning my lips.

My gaze drops to his parted lips, and butterflies wreak havoc in my stomach. Warmth pools in my lower belly and spreads through my core, and even I can smell my own arousal scenting the air around us. Zoltan's fangs lengthen as I watch, the sharp points denting the pillowy skin on his lower lip. An entirely different groan rumbles in his chest, reflecting through my own body. It's enough to jerk me away from him.

"You should be okay." I sound breathy, my voice huskier than usual, but I push through the nerves forcing me to blubber. "Your pupils look normal, not dilated. I mean, there is nothing normal about them, they look like freaking suns. Who the hell has suns in their eyes, right? But for a freak like you... I meant to say for a Daywalker, that's normal." Giving him a sharp nod, I pet his chest like stroking a horse's ass, none too gently. "I did not damage you apart from bruising your jewels, which I should remind you that you agreed it was deserved." Realizing I'm still slapping his pecs, I snatch my hand away.

"I told you she is weird when she's nervous," Fenrir murmurs to Cassius somewhere behind Zoltan's back.

Using the Fae as an escape, I round on him, shouldering my way past Zoltan. He doesn't move, so I kind of struggle around him, bouncing off his side and stumbling towards the Fae. Cassius looks ready to cry, his face as red as a tomato as he bites his mouth to stop himself from laughing.

He is a smart man.

"Who the hell made you an expert on Francesca Drake?" Scowling down my nose at Fenrir, my fists slam on my hips.

"I'm not, but at least I gave Zoltan a moment to wrestle

his control back." Jerking his chin, the Fae points behind me. "He was ready to turn full predator mode, and I'm not really sure you are ready to see him like that yet."

Feeling like an idiot, I don't dare to turn and look over my shoulder. Awareness curdles the blood in my veins like milk gone bad. Feeling Zoltan's attention on me raises the small hairs on the back of my neck. Unwilling to show how much this whole situation unnerved me, I nod sharply at Fenrir and walk back to the armchair, avoiding the vampire's gaze.

Zoltan tracks my movement.

"As I said, all of you are insane if you think what you just told me will convince me to stay here and help you out." Now that I'm facing the other two, I notice that the Fae has turned his body fully towards me while Cassius looks ready to spring and tackle Zoltan.

A stupid part of my brain dares the sinful vampire to pounce on me. It's not a surprise since I always act like I have a death wish. It's a known fact.

"I don't think he will attack me." Saying it to no one in particular, I know I speak the truth. "I'm not afraid of him."

"Stay quiet, Francesca...please." Fenrir pleads with his eyes as well as his words. "Zoltan is the most dangerous of all of us when his control slips. Not even the Board dares to provoke him. It's one of the reasons we are still breathing while poking where we shouldn't."

"You are scaring her more." Zoltan's voice sounds strained as he stiffly walks away, sitting back in his chair. "I don't think that will help our case."

Cassius looks from Zoltan to me and back, not able to cover the shock on his face fast enough. I guess he expected a bloodbath or something. Now that I feel how easily the air slides in and out of my lungs, I understand fully the peculiar situation I created. The tension lifting from the air makes me feel weightless for a moment.

"So, I don't understand." Getting Fenrir's attention, I push everything else aside. "You have been doing this for a while. The Board, whoever they are, will not go against Zoltan, and you still think I can help you with something?"

"The Board doesn't think it's smart to provoke Zoltan. There is a difference." With a sigh, the Fae shifts uneasily. "We can't access the archives to see who has been visiting Sienna." Fenrir doesn't look happy admitting this.

"Okay." Dragging the word out slowly, I wait for the rest.

"I think you will be able to access it." Fenrir stiffens for a second but shakes it off, hopefully getting to his point before I do more stupid stuff. "Zoltan disagreed with me for a long time." Avoiding my gaze, Fenrir stares at my forehead, I almost think I'm growing a horn.

Finally, his words register in my brain.

"Wait a minute." The Fae clenches his jaw, pissing me off. "How long has he disagreed with you?" More importantly, I want him to tell me how long he's been watching me.

"Five years." Fenrir opens his mouth, but Cassius answers. "She needs to know the truth," Ignoring Fenrir's glare, the large man looks me dead in the eyes. "Five years we couldn't agree if it would be smart to bring you here. Then Roberti's name started being mentioned too often for our liking around here. Zoltan was the last to agree." Glancing at the vampire, Cassius sighs. "He agreed not a full week ago."

Wracking my brain, I'm trying to piece the timeline together. I can't remember anything important happening five years ago that would bring their attention to me. The last week, however, is a totally different story. I've been here two days already, and I was stewing in misery for four days before that because I got suspended. That is six days right there. The seventh, marking the full week, is when I was chasing the shifter through the streets of Sienna, and I saw those shadows.

My gaze locks on Fenrir. "You know about the shadows." If my words sound like an accusation, that's because they are.

"What shadows?" There is no way he could be acting. The confusion clouding his features is too genuine.

"He doesn't know." Zoltan's voice makes me look at him finally.

Dread, mixed with some feeling I can't name right now, pools in my stomach.

"But you do." It's not a question because the puzzle has come together, and it numbs my lips.

"I do." There is not an ounce of apology on the vampire's face.

"It was you that night, wasn't it? The one who saved me from it?" Not waiting for confirmation—not that there was going to be one—I push through, speaking my thoughts out loud. "You saw me that night, followed me as I was going after the shifter. That's when you changed your mind and decided to agree with them."

One small nod is all I get as he watches my face unblinking, daring me to say anything else. Fenrir, oblivious to the tension, rising up around us again, clears his throat.

"I was coming to at least get some of your blood the night I saw you at the bar." Looking sheepish, he shrugs. "I wasn't expecting you to be so… unfriendly." I'm sure the word unfriendly was not his first choice.

"What does my blood have to do with all this?" I feel like screaming. Every time one thing becomes clear, they add in some other nonsense.

"We believe with the right blood, you can access the archives," Cassius mumbles.

"You think my blood is the key? They already have enough half-bloods. Doesn't the Board have access to the records? It doesn't make sense."

"The academy is built on ancient magic we don't understand. Only one member of the Board knows the truth, but he is so old that most of the time, the words coming out of his mouth are not even in a language any of us understand. The academy itself, using magic"—Fenrir clarifies, pausing for effect, I guess— " keeps a record of who is coming and going through the wards. None of us can access it."

"And did you?" When the Fae looks at me with a frown, I ask the full question. "Did you get any of my blood?"

"Of course not. You wouldn't let me near you, remember?" Scoffing, Fenrir waves a hand. "It wasn't too important. Cassius called as soon as you left the bar, telling me Zoltan agreed. I contacted Roberti immediately, setting it up for you to arrive as fast as possible."

Turning my accusing stare from the Fae to Zoltan, I force my jaw to unclench itself. "He didn't get my blood, but you did."

"I did." My heart is jackhammering at his arrogant, and unapologetic stare. "I had to make sure your blood was different from all traces left by the others that went missing."

"And was it?" I know the answer, but I can't help myself.

"It was."

"Let's just be grateful she hasn't bled all over the place here." Fenrir's comment screeches everything to a halt.

"What?" Glancing from me to Zoltan, the Fae pales. "It was just a drop, and you took it Zoltan." Mentioning the fight with the demon guard and the ghoul, the accusation hangs in the air.

I know my ears were bleeding when I entered the academy grounds through the forest because my clothing is still stained from it when that horrible sound brought me to my knees. So that's why Zoltan grabbed me, taking me out of the open as fast as his feet would carry him. There was no blood on my face, my neck, or my hands when I got to Fenrir's room, which tells me the vampire cleaned me up while I was numb from pain. I can see him searching his memory while we stare at each other.

"I'm certain she didn't bleed on the soil." He does not sound sure at all.

My stomach lurches.

"Fenrir!" Argoz's bellow makes me jump a foot off the chair. "I have wonderful news!" Rushing over to us, the ghoul claps his hands happily. "The Board is having a party in two days to welcome your mate. Isn't that the best news we've had in a long time?"

"I could be wrong." Zoltan continues our conversation about me bleeding on the academy grounds, ignoring Argoz, who is still wired with excitement.

"Best news, indeed," Fenrir answers the ghoul in a flat voice, sending dread to the bottom of my soul.

Chapter Twenty

The vast space with its high ceilings, feels oppressive and stifling. My rib cage tightens painfully under my skin as if wanting to crush my lungs and heart while I watch the excitement drain from the ghoul's face. If the last two days are anything to go by in this place, I can't begrudge him his happiness at the idea of a party. I would be too, honestly. Being able to let loose and push the stress and worry aside for a moment is quite tempting, but with my life on the line, the idea of fun just isn't working for me.

"I feel like I'm missing something." Argoz turns from Zoltan to Fenrir to Cassius, a frown pulling his eyebrows low over his eyes. "I don't like it."

"We were telling Francesca about the problems with the humans and the portal." Cassius is the first to recover from the stunned silence. "I felt it important for her to be aware of the danger since she will be here for a while longer." Elaborating, when the ghoul opens his mouth to argue, he waves for him to take a seat.

"On whose authority do you divulge crucial information

about this institution? This"—Argoz's hand swivels in my direction, encompassing my persona— "is not a typical situation. She is one of very few that will exit those gates. What exactly are the three of you trying to do? Get us all killed?" Jaw clenching and fists balling, he refuses the offered seat.

"Be it a day, or a lifetime, if the roles were reversed, you wouldn't want to know?" Cassius challenges, the yellow eye narrowing slightly. "If it were my daughter, I know I would look favorably to whoever warned her."

"But she is not your daughter. She is a guest, not yet bound as a mate to a Daywalker." Argoz winces noticeably, and I look from him to Cassius, not understanding his reaction.

"And we know how much being bound to one of us can save a life, don't we?" Although it was spoken casually, the pain and resentment are hard to miss in Cassius's voice.

My lips part, the question surging up, sitting on the tip of my tongue, but Fenrir shakes his head slightly, stopping my words. I want to know. I need to know if the large man has lost his mate, if she perished here, and why she lost her life. Some crazy part of my brain prods at me insistently, as if it's of utmost importance in this otherwise horrible situation. Or I might just be looking for a distraction from my own doomed fate. Respecting the warning the Fae gave me, fingers gouging holes in my shirt, I swallow the question. And through all this, Zoltan sits as still as a statue, his unreadable gaze entirely centered on me. I can't deal with this.

It's too much, too fast.

Hoisting myself off the armchair, I stop for a second, seeing Argoz jerk away from me. Maybe I jumped up a bit too fast. My ego would've been stroked by him getting defensive if I didn't feel freaked out and dead inside at the same time. Being here with them, with everything sitting on top of me like an anvil suffocating me slowly, is almost akin to torture. I need time away from it all. Time to think without any of them following on my heels.

"I need to walk off some energy. I will be back." Avoiding their gazes, I step away with my head held high.

"You need an escort…" I can tell Fenrir is already on his feet behind me without turning around.

"Let her go." Zoltan's voice carries through the space, and my feet only speed up.

Walking as fast as I can without it turning into a jog, their voices get more distant until I can't hear them anymore. The hum from the dining hall disappears too, and I wander aimlessly through the building, the surroundings blurring into a fog. I thought that I wanted to think things through, but my head feels empty. Not even a stray word passes through my mind while my unseeing eyes stare ahead.

Twice I find myself turning around and walking away with difficulty from the hallways decorated in golden accents. Even when I feel numb, the pull at the center of my chest is like a hook lodged deep inside, railing me towards it. It might be the danger or some ingrained sense of self-preservation that jerks me out of the daze as soon as I find myself in front of it. Not wanting to tempt fate, I head for the opposite side of the building. Out of sight, out of mind.

People pass me, their faces foggy, and I'm grateful that I don't bump into anyone crossing my path. Not that I would know if I did. I know nothing and feel even less right now.

"What did you get yourself into this time, Franky?" My lips are so numb they barely move.

I realize I have exited the building the moment a cool breeze ruffles the hairs that have escaped my braid, and they float around my face, tickling it. Blinking fast, my vision clears, showing me the vast open space surrounding the academy, the forest stretching in the distance. Yellow eyes pop out in the darkness, guards of demons and shifters prowling the grounds. That same ancient magic I felt when I came here prods at me, like a tentative caress on my skin. My heart does a painful thump against my ribs, and a shiver like ghostly fingers trails up my spine.

I want to turn around and run back inside where I'll be safe. Where this ancient thing that even the Daywalkers can't understand won't find me and try to lure me with its gentle touches. My feet inch forwards, the sound of crunching gravel following like a cheerleader in my wake. Energy churns inside me, spreading through my limbs, and my fingers tingle as if they are coming to life after being numb for too long. The humorless laugh passing my lips sounds too strange to my own ears, yet I keep walking, powerless to do anything but answer the call.

The sound of tires crushing the uneven ground pulls me out of it, breaking the connection and snapping me out of the trance. With my chest rising and falling because of my fast breathing, my eyes dart around, finally seeing the silvery blanket the pregnant moon casts on everything around me. Dread overrides all other feelings when I know that I've walked almost halfway to the accursed forest where her damn traps are waiting to end me the moment I step foot inside the trees. What am I even doing here when I know now that I was intentionally lured for some crazy plans three Daywalkers have cooked up?

That ludicrous thought that the building itself is safe was simply insanity talking, as well. No place on these grounds is safe for me, and I need to find a way to get the hell out of here. Roberti needs to know what is going on. I have no doubt he will find a solution and fix this. He always does. No matter how much I've screwed up and how bad I test his patience, Andrius Roberti has protected me most of my life.

He will protect me now, too.

That thought does not sound as assured and as comforting as it used to. The one person that I know I can turn to for help doesn't bring the same assurance I always get at the times I feel I'm in a tight spot. All these people plotting around my life have made me paranoid. It's the only comfort I can give myself as I burst through the large open doors, stumbling inside the academy panting while trying to inhale short breaths. With my hands on my knees, I ignore the strange looks the few passersby give me as I catch my breath. I hope all of them will go away and disappear so I can be alone.

Not wanting to stay here long in case Fenrir decides I've had enough free reign, with trembling legs, I take the wide stairway two at a time to the upper levels on my right. If nothing else, it will at least take the Fae longer until he can find me. Perking up slightly at the thought, I breathe in the scents of herbs and incense that saturate the air on the second floor, not staying long enough to fully enjoy them as I continue climbing up.

The third floor smells like misty books and ink on paper, the scent bringing me peace like nothing else. Inhaling it deeply, my feet slow down when I look around to take it all in. Releasing the curved banister I've been using to pull myself up, my feet barely touch the floor as I gingerly explore the level. Many doors stand closed on either side, even across the open space on the opposite side of the building. No heartbeat or sound can be heard, and I find myself stopping at a large arched window, the sill extending inwards and wide enough for me to take a seat. Not willing to allow myself to get in more trouble, like opening one of the doors and causing some disaster no doubt, I climb on it. Propping my chin on top of my knees and hugging my chest, I stare at the moon in the cloudless sky.

The silver glow streams through the glass, bathing my face. Flames dance around me on the walls, their orangey glow combined with the calming scent relaxing my coiled-up muscles, and I sag deeper into my hidey hole. Closing my eyes, I tilt my face to the side so I can feel more of the moon on my skin. With a deep sigh, I can't help but wonder how the sun might feel against my skin, the bright warm rays gliding over me and warming me like nothing ever has.

What's it like to be a Daywalker?

Even though I'll never admit it out loud, I've always wondered.

I wished…

Wishing for what you can't have is one way to get killed in our world. And now, knowing what I know, I can't help but ponder if it's worth it. If all these people would still risk their lives and be here if they knew they might die. What would push them to the point that death would be worth tempting so you could walk the day? Am I missing something? What do all of them know that I don't? Life is not bad in Sienna, and I'm saying that as a half blood. It's even better for a pure blood. You can have the life you want, with any carrier that you want to build.

And live in darkness.

If I was a pure blood, would I have been willing to face death and trade my immortality for the bright skies and warm sun? *Isn't that what you are doing now even with inadequate genes?* I push that snarky thought away, but the answer is still there, nonetheless.

Probably.

Lost in thought, my body stiffens when I feel the electric charge in the air around me. My skin prickles like a million tiny needles stabbing my every pore. With the small hairs standing on end at the back of my neck, I take a deep breath, praying for a miracle, squeezing my eyes shut tight. Maybe if I was a half mage, I could wish him away. But I won't, and he is getting closer by the second. My whole body tunes into his presence, soaking it up like a dried-up sponge. There is no need to see him to know who he is. My body recognizes him from a mile away, perking up like a stupid fool unaware of what he represents to me.

Certain death.

You don't get to lay with a beast that can't be tamed and expect to survive it. If your physical body does not die, your soul will be crushed and ripped to pieces, leaving you begging to meet your end. And I know he will do that to me, yet my foolish heart sputters like the wings of a dying butterfly when I feel his gaze on the crown of my head.

"You shouldn't have come." My words are barely above a whisper.

He says nothing, just as I expected.

Lifting my head up, I finally open my eyes to look at him.

Zoltan.

Leaning his shoulder on the edge of the window, his deep blue eyes look black in the candlelight. Shadows dance across his handsome face, making my fingers twitch with the need to reach up and trace them across his high cheekbones and full lips. He doesn't move or say anything. Those eyes of his just stare to the very depths of my soul, as if daring me to run. Or worse, to answer the call that I felt the moment my gaze connected with his. Hell, even sooner than that. The moment I saw the outline of him in the middle of the dirty street in Sienna when Daywalker Academy was just a stone building in the distance looming over our lives.

"You shouldn't have come." Repeating the words, my mouth dries out, making it difficult to speak.

"I know." His nostrils flare, and his jaw sets with determination.

Chapter Twenty-One

"What are you doing?"

Panic makes me sound like a scared little girl when he pushes off the wall and steps closer. Heart jackhammering in my chest, stomach rolling with frenzied butterflies, I stare at him wide-eyed. My mind screams at me to push him away, to run and hide, or even break the window and jump headfirst from the third floor. Anything but allowing him to close the distance.

Yet, I stay frozen, like a deer in headlights, paralyzed by his smoldering gaze. Dizziness makes me lightheaded, and when his hand lifts up, cupping my face, my body sways towards him, pressing his palm firmer against my skin. A current passes from his hand through my entire body, sinking its claws inside me. I want to yell at him, accuse him of messing with my head, but I know it to be a lie. He is not using his powers or gifts on me right now. No. My reaction is entirely my own fault, and probably a result of my idiocy.

I don't value my life.

"You are afraid of me." Zoltan's rough thumb scrapes

the skin on my cheekbone while he strokes it gently, his gaze searching mine.

"Shouldn't I be?" Sounding breathless is better than being unable to speak.

Nodding slightly, he doesn't release me from his hold. "If you are smart, you should be."

"I'm not." Blurting the words out without thinking, all I can do is blink at his raised eyebrow.

"You do not fear me?" A look passes through his eyes too fast for my mentally distressed brain to catch.

"I'm not smart." Swallowing the lump the size of a fist in my throat, I give him a sheepish look. "I still fear you."

"You should give yourself more credit, Francesca Drake." His lips quirk at the corners, and I shiver from the way my name rolls off his tongue.

He is standing too close, his large warm palm cradling my cheek, and that damn thumb keeps gliding, the roughness of it catching slightly on my skin with each stroke. I feel it in all the inappropriate places, so much so it feels like he is touching me there and not innocently petting my face. The heat of his body burns my skin, goosebumps covering my arms and legs while ants are crawling up my spine. He knows exactly what he is doing to me, and his barely contained smirk gives that fact away.

I should slap him.

"I'll do it."

The words coming out of my mouth shock me more than they do him. Blinking rapidly, I want to take them back, but my mouth refuses to open. His thumb stops moving over my cheekbone, his fingers tighten around my face, and his eyes begin to glow. I'm not sure if I made the decision subconsciously while wandering aimlessly through the place, or I just wanted to break the enchantment that his nearness casts over me.

"You don't have to. I came here to tell you that I will help you leave." His deep voice sounds like a distant boom of thunder rumbling in his chest.

It's a beautiful thing to hear, even though it's bullshit and we both know it. I went outside these walls. I felt the pull the magic that has taken ownership of this place has on me. There is no leaving for me, not right now at least. But there is one crucial thing that I need to know.

"Why did you agree for me to be lured here?" Rubbing the center of my chest to lessen the pain my fast beating heart is inflicting in hopes of escaping my ribcage, I don't shy away from his penetrating gaze.

His attention drops from my eyes to the hand pressed between my breasts, his chest bumping my still curled-up legs when he steps even closer. Zoltan, intentionally or not, has me caged between the window and his body, leaving me surprised that I don't panic or start swinging at his head. Wetness dampens my panties, my core pulsing with the beat of my heart. In reaction, his nostrils flare more, and his gaze snaps back to my face.

"The only way I can protect you is if you are close to me." It sounds like gibberish to me, and after a long moment of staring at the hunger on his face, the words begin to make sense.

"Why in the world would you care?" When his lips press in a thin line, I laugh humorlessly. "You don't know me from Adam, Zoltan. Why the fuck would you care what happens to me?"

"Such crude words from such a pretty mouth." One side of his mouth tilts up, and although my nipples tighten and my girly bits start tingling happily, I see it for what it is.

"Why?" I don't let him sidetrack me.

"I knew Adam, and he wasn't all that important." The offhanded comment sends my head spinning, trying to calculate just how old he is. Lucky that I'm sitting down because I might've dropped on my ass, his next words save me from attacking him with questions. "There is something about you, Francesca. And I have every intention of staying close until I figure out what that is."

The comment sounds so close to what Roberti said to me what feels like a lifetime ago. That night when he found me bathed in blood from head to toe, barely resembling a sentient being, with bodies scattered around the room. The night I signed my fate of becoming an agent, which in return led me here. My mouth hangs open while I stare mutely at the vampire.

"That is something every girl loves to hear, but"— Lifting a finger in his face, I snatch it back when the tips of his fangs make an appearance— "there is nothing special about me. I'm a half blood that should be grateful I survived this long."

"We will agree to disagree on this, fledgling." Chuckling, he looks pointedly where I'm hugging the finger that was in his face a second ago.

"Nowhere near a fledgling." Saying it slowly as if he's stupid, I point at myself, "Half-blood. That's all I am."

"And that's where you are wrong, Miss Drake." His hand tilts my face up. "You are so much more than that, and I will find all your secrets."

His face is close enough for me to still hold his gaze without crossing my eyes. It's difficult to breathe while I watch his eyes turn, the pupils spreading like tiny suns through his irises. The silver glow of the moon turns the blue color into melted steel, allowing me to see my reflection staring back at me with parted lips. My tongue pokes out, wetting them, and Zoltan groans deep in his throat, pulling slightly away. I hate when he is so close, but I miss him when he isn't… Conflicting emotions rage a war inside me, and some of it must've shown on my face. His eyes soften, no less smoldering than they usually are, but it's easier to breathe.

"You will survive this, Francesca. I'll make sure of it." It sounds more like an oath than a promise, sending a tremor through my limbs. "Drink now."

"Huh?" Not a very articulate reaction, but there you have it.

"I said drink." Moving his hand slightly, his wrist presses on my lips. "You need it. This land has not fully accepted you yet. It's draining you slowly, and you'll need all the strength you can get."

If I were standing, I would've fallen with the push of a finger. Offering blood was not something supernaturals do lightly. Something Fenrir learned the hard way, I think. A vampire offering his blood, Daywalker at that, is unheard of. They are well known for taking, not for their giving nature. And the most stupefying thing is not even that. It's the fact that I want to push his wrist away and sink my fangs in his neck.

Another pained groan comes from Zoltan, and I realize I'm staring at the pulsing vein on his neck like I'm in bloodlust. Embarrassment makes me drop my gaze, and I squeeze my eyes shut, unwilling to see the gloating look on his face. I really am pathetic.

"Look at me." His voice is rough, his words husky and low. "Look at me, Francesca."

Steeling my spine, I allow him to lift my head. My breath catches in my throat at the intensity on his face. He looks like he is a hairsbreadth away from pouncing on me, his entire body rigid as he fights to stay in control.

"I want nothing more than to have your mouth on me and your fangs deep in my neck." If he keeps talking, I wonder if an immortal can die from a heart attack. By the sound of my heart hammering away, I think I'm willing to try. "But I cannot promise I will be able to hold back and not sink mine into you. Right now, my control is holding by a thread after the last two days, and I don't trust myself to stop when it's needed. So, take the wrist tonight and stop looking at me that way. Do not push me, woman, for I am not that strong."

With my heart in my throat, and my whole body quaking from his words, my trembling fingers wrap around his wrist. Holding him like a cup, I let my lips graze his skin before the sharp tips of my fangs pierce him. A deep moan could not be stopped when his precious blood fills my mouth and slides down my throat. Closing my eyes so I don't watch the hunger on his face, I drink greedily even though I don't need to feed right now. His fingers wrap my braid around his hand, and he presses me harder to his wrist as if I'm trying to escape. He must be insane because I'm not sure I'll be able to stop before I drain him dry.

Too soon, my head is wrenched back, Zoltan yanking on my braid and tearing the skin on his wrist when I don't unfuse my mouth fast enough. My eyes fly open just in time to see his descending on me with a feral look twisting his handsome features. Crushing his lips to mine in a bruising kiss, his blood that I didn't manage to swallow fills both our mouths. My hands fly to his shoulders, clawing at him, trying to bring him closer. His arms wrap around me like a steel vice pressing me to his chest, and his tongue invades my mouth, twisting and curling around mine.

Shifting on the windowsill, I turn to face him, wrapping my legs around his hips, pulling him as close as I can. Zoltan's hand still has my braid wrapped around it, and he uses it to move me how he wants so he can deepen the kiss. This doesn't feel like an urge, or even a lust-fueled instinct. He holds me trapped, not that I'm trying to escape, devouring me with his lips alone. It feels monumental.

A claiming.

His thick erection hits the right spot between my legs, and all thoughts disappear from my head. Like horny teenagers, we grind against each other, my wetness without a doubt drenching both our clothing. My greedy fingers sink into his hair, pulling on the silky strands just like I wanted to do from the moment I saw him. Tugging on my braid, he sucks on my tongue, his other hand trailing down my back before grabbing my ass and pressing me harder against his cock.

Stars burst behind my eyes, and I spasm in his arms, my body shaking and almost dislodging him from me. Zoltan grips me harder, his loud growl mixing with my moans and mewls. An eternity later, I finally sag against his chest, his lips trailing kisses over my face and neck. Pressing my face at his throat, I hide my embarrassment for my behavior, but this is Zoltan we are talking about. He will not let me hide from anything—not even myself.

Pulling back, he looks down at me, his face relaxed for the first time since I met him. Crinkles form at the corners of his eyes before he places a tiny peck on the tip of my nose. I know I'm staring, but I can't help myself. He looks so normal. Well, as normal as a very old and powerful Daywalker can look at any rate.

"That should be enough for now."

Kissing my forehead, he rearranges me back on the

windowsill. I allow it, too stunned to speak until I realize he is talking about the blood, not the orgasm he just gave me. Speaking of which, I can feel my face turning all shades of red and getting hot enough to burn anyone who touches it. As subtle as I can be, I glance at his crotch to see if I have made a patch on his pants. Another thing to add to the depraved actions of Francesca Drake for the night.

My jaw hits my chest when my eyes land between his legs. I know I was wet as hell, and I can feel my pants sticking to my thighs, but no way in hell I made that much mess on my own. My eyes snap to Zoltan's face, and if I expected embarrassment to match mine, I was sorely disappointed. Hunger still lurks in his gaze, but there is something else there too. Something I will do everything to ignore right now.

Zoltan leans closer, his lips pressing on mine too fast to count before he pulls back. Intentionally, his hand goes to the large wet patch on his pants, and he adjusts himself before pulling his shirt out of the waistband and letting it drop over it. I watch stunned, still gaping like a fish when he smirks and winks before walking away.

"I will see you in the morning, Miss Drake. Meet me at the weapons room, as you call it." Speaking without turning back, he saunters away from me. "And, Francesca...don't make me come looking for you."

I stare at the last trace of his back before he rounds a corner. The fact that I let Zoltan grope me out in the open is shocking. The fact he looked smug for cumming in his pants is as crazed as it is exuberating.

Chapter Twenty-Two

"I hate you!" Glaring at the asshole vampire, I push up on my forearms so he can see my face better.

In case he didn't hear me yelling at him.

I stupidly listen to Zoltan and show up at the weapons room. That was yesterday morning. It's been over twenty-four hours, and I haven't slept, rested, or left this cursed room since. Apparently, the crazy man thinks he can teach me how to resist a mind fuck by the time of the party. I started referring to it as the funeral. I have no delusions of how slim my chances of survival are.

Unlike Zoltan.

He lives in a world of his own where unicorns are skipping rainbows, and everyone lives happily ever after. Well, not really. Unless the unicorns are some scary man-eating beasts that will stab everyone on their barb wired horns, but you get my point.

He thinks I'll live.

I strongly disagree.

"Stop wasting time, Miss Drake." Barking at me, he kicks my foot. "Get your ass up."

If I expect things to be awkward when we see each other next, or fates forbid for the jerk to show a sweet or a soft side, I would be disappointed. It isn't awkward because overnight he turns from a scary beast into a drill Sergeant. Humping might not have been something he is familiar with because I have strong suspicions that it short-circuited his brain. As I'm watching his frown from my sprawled position on the floor where I spend the majority of my time since I enter this room, I can't decide which Zoltan I like better. The arrogant beast, or the frustrating jerk.

"I still think you are trying to punish me for something." Grumbling, I push off the floor. "This is absolutely unnecessary, and it looks more like wasting time than doing something productive. Like trying to get into the archives."

"The archives will be there after the party. If you can't block out mind control, you may not be." The ever-helpful Fenrir chirps from his corner where he's been sitting and enjoying my torment for hours.

"I should've drained your ass when I had the chance." Fenrir frowns uneasily, but it's Zoltan's reaction I was going for.

And…there it is.

Jaw clenching, I can hear his teeth grinding all the way where I'm finally standing on my throbbing feet. Grinning at him like an idiot, I lift an eyebrow, daring him to open his mouth. If he wants to pretend he didn't mess me up for the rest of my life with just a kiss, I can piss him off as much as I want. I'm mature like that.

The mental punch he sends my way doubles me over. Groaning and gripping my knees for all I'm worth, I try my best to block him out. Imagining walls made of bricks did not work. Closing doors, or hell, even raising steel walls couldn't block his assaults. No matter what he tells me to try, I'm like an open field left for him to plow through. I can feel tears streaming down my face, the pain unbearable, but he doesn't let go. I know he won't until I'm almost passed out on the floor. I learned his tricks early yesterday.

"There you are." A smooth female voice purrs happily, but I'm in so much pain I can't lift my head to see who it is.

Fenrir groans somewhere in the room, and I wonder if Zoltan decided to hit him a little too. It'll serve the Fae right for sitting there watching me suffer and enjoying every minute of it. Steeling myself for another mental punch—it's a pattern Zoltan has—I almost fall flat on my face when the pressure totally disappears. It lasts longer than a heartbeat, and I finally lift my head up, flicking the hair off my face.

I wish I stayed in crippling pain instead of seeing a beautiful woman wrapped around Zoltan like a boa that's trying to strangle her prey. My heart does a painful lurch when she presses her face in his neck, and his arms wrap lovingly around her body, while his gaze is locked on mine. Fenrir gasps and starts yapping something, but his words blur into nothing. Pain like nothing Zoltan could've mentally inflicted stabs me at the center of my chest, and I'm shocked to see I'm not crumpled on the ground bleeding out. What are seconds seem like days as I watch them entwined around each other. The woman has her eyes closed, oblivious of everyone but the man holding her in his arms.

The same arms that were wrapped around me.

Realization dawns on Zoltan's face, maybe from finally understanding the situation or seeing something on my blood-drained face, and his hand moves to reach for me. Something inside me snaps. A crippling fear that he might force me to stand here and continue to watch them together. Or worse, convincing me it's not what I think it is because I know I'm stupid enough to believe him. The energy surges through my limbs, and I feel the blast bursting from my chest and sending both of them flying back, slamming into the opposite wall and falling in an unmoving heap on the floor. Fenrir's droning words are silent, and one glance at him shows me he is on the ground too, his long, platinum hair fanned around his head. Shocked, I stand frozen in the silent room while looking wide eyed from one unconscious person to the next. When Zoltan is the first to move, his arms flinching before he tries to roll to his side, I bolt out of there so fast that a few people passing the door end up bowled down like pins.

"Francesca!" Zoltan's bellow sends me running faster.

The fat tears overflowing my eyes make everything blurry while I streak through the academy. With no destination in mind, I'm not even surprised when I see the hallways decorated with golden accents getting closer and closer. The pain in my chest starts spreading wider, numbing my lungs and my heart. My hair flying behind me like a flag, I'm not sure if I'm running away from Zoltan, or I'm trying to outrun the crippling feeling overtaking my body and soul.

What did you think? That he was yours to keep? The snarky comment in my head was unwelcomed and a much-needed reminder of how stupid I am.

The calling of my name disappears along with the rest of the sound that is a constant buzz in the building the moment my feet enter the alluring hallway. My skin prickles just like when I pass through wards when I enter it without slowing down my speed. Even here, I can feel the damn vampire, his energy reaching for me like a spiderweb trying to trap me and reel me back to him.

I will not let it.

My lips are bleeding from biting on them as hard as I can to stop the sobs from escaping. I didn't cry apart from a few treacherous tears when my father was killed, so I will most assuredly not cry for a fucking man I've known for not even a week. Doors blur as I keep running through the seemingly endless hallway until I'm forced to stop in front of a closed door at a dead end. Sucking lungfuls of air, my eyes dart around as if Zoltan can materialize at any moment. My head jerks back, looking over my shoulder when scuffing on the floor alerts me to someone sneaking in. I might be hallucinating, but I'm not willing to wait and see if I'm right. Grabbing the golden handle of the door in front of me, I yank it open, stepping inside and slamming it closed behind me. Pressing my back on it, I close my eyes while I breathe deeply in hopes to slow down my heart.

As soon as my lids drop, I can see them together. Both of them dark, tall, beautiful together, their bodies wrapped around each other so that nothing can pull them apart. Another stab, this one more painful than the first, doubles me over, and I drop to my knees at the door. Loud sobs are wrenched from the bottom of my soul, and there is nothing I can do to stop them. Pressing my forehead on the soft floor, I hug my middle as I cry like I've never done before. My tears drench the thick carpet, but it dries out by the time only sniffles and tremors are making my body twitch. Spent and numb, I drop on my side, staring with glazed over eyes at nothing. Even the reason that brought me here in this state is gone from my mind.

I feel nothing.

"That was quite a display," a frail voice speaks, but I have no strength to move apart from blinking. "If I knew a boy will force you to come to me after I've spent days trying to call you here, I would've forced his hand to kiss you sooner."

That got my attention, alright.

Jerking upright, my head swivels around to find the owner of the voice. The room is empty, sending shivers down my spine. *You are so stupid, Franky. Running here like an idiot without thinking.*

"What's new?" my voice is raspy, and my throat hurts when I answer my inner voice like I've been screaming for weeks.

"I don't know, why don't you tell me, child?" The frail voice chuckles softly.

"I wasn't talking to you." Massaging my throat as if that will help, I push myself off the floor.

"It's just you and me here."

"Thanks, Mr. Obvious."

"My name is Soren; I don't know Obvious." Whoever it is, sounds thoughtful. I almost laugh. Almost. "It has been a while since I have been outside these rooms. Is he a new one? Do we have a new Daywalker?"

"Where are you, Soren?" Ignoring his question, I inch further into the room. "Why can't I see you?"

The place would be pitch black if it weren't for the slightly-parted drapes on the windows, which let the silver glow of the moon break the darkness. Shadows seem like they loom in every corner, and I almost jump out of my skin when a lump moves on top of the large bed at the center of the room. The rushing of my blood through my veins sounds like a train in my ears.

"Come closer, let me see you." The lump moves again, the blankets covering it stretching like an eggshell preparing to burst open.

It's creepy as hell, and I'm not surprised when goose-bumps raise over my arms.

"Why did you need me to come here?" Sliding my feet slowly, I move closer still. "Was that you making that irresistible pull that lured me in the hallway?"

"It was." He chuckles happily. "I thought I lost my touch when you didn't come."

"Has no one told you that in these new times, we actually call people using words? It's creepy and deranged otherwise to lure them in like a predator."

"No one comes here anymore." Sad and petulant, he moves again under the blankets, and I crane my neck to see him from this far away with no luck. "They have forgotten who keeps all of them alive."

My stomach drops to my feet at that statement.

"You control the ancient magic of this place?" Hissing angrily, I grab control of my anger until I hear more of what he has to say.

If he is the one doing all the killings here and in Sienna, only one of us will be left breathing in this room by the time I'm done. The energy that knocked over everyone in the weapons room starts churning in my chest, spreading through my limbs. My heartbeat slows down, the gentle feeling washing over me like a soothing balm.

Thump.

"Oh, how powerful you are going to be." Still chuckling, Soren talks, oblivious that I'm about to rip his throat with my bare hands if he answers one question wrong.

"Are you the one killing the students and the residents of Sienna?"

"Of course not." Scoffing, he twists again under the damn blanket.

"You said you keep everyone alive. Are you controlling

the ancient magic of the academy?" Asking the question he didn't answer, I move closer a foot.

"Control it?" Confusion is evident in his frail voice. "No, nothing can control the magic child. I only feed it."

Thump.

"You what?" I sound shrill, but he shocks me so much I take a step back, snapping out of the trance-like state I was in.

"Any existing magic has to feed on a life source. For the academy to stand, someone had to feed it. I was the one that took on the task." Flipping again, he finally stops twisting. "Not that they are grateful, the ignorant fools."

"Why did you want me to come here, Soren?" Taking another step back, my knees bend, preparing to attack him if he is trying to trick me by acting harmless. "Do you need to feed so you can fuel the magic, too? Is that why you were pulling me here?"

"What nonsense are you speaking, child?" Soren's voice sounds stronger in his anger at my insult. "I was calling you here so I can help you survive."

"Survive what? The party?" My hands drop slightly in confusion. Maybe Soren is crazy and has no idea what he is talking about.

"What party?" A cough rakes him, and he continues to mutter about parties and no one inviting him anywhere anymore. I stand with my mouth open. "You need to survive this place if we are to remove the plague that is spreading on our grounds. You need my help or all the world will be cast in darkness."

"Why do you care if I live or die? I'm no one; I can barely look after myself, much less the rest of the world. You got the wrong girl, buddy."

Shaking my head, I almost turn to walk away. This is all

stupid. I want to find a hole and hide for a decade to lick my wounds. I can't even take a break in peace in this damn place.

"I know I have the right girl. It's you that can't see it," Soren says so softly I nearly miss it.

"I'm not even supposed to be here, Soren!" The hurt, frustration, and anger make me want to scream, so I snap at him. "I'm a fucking half-blood in the middle of your fucking glorious Daywalker academy."

"You are more than that, Francesca Drake."

"I need everyone to stop using that cheesy line!"

"But I know it to be true."

Soren is persistent, pissing me off so bad that I storm next to his bedside without thinking. A frail, thin man with long, white hair lays peacefully at the center of the bed, his eyes closed and his dried lips lifted at the corners in a serene smile. He looks Fae, but his ears are covered, so I can't be sure. The blue veins are visible through his pale, paper-thin skin, yet his face is unlined, and no wrinkles can be seen. His head turns slightly as if he can feel me watching him.

"How can you be so sure, Soren?"

"Because you are just like me, Francesca." His eyes snap open, and my entire world screeches to a halt.

Snake eyes are staring back at me, and the world turns dark.

Chapter Twenty-Three

Flattening the invisible wrinkles on the silky red camisole that magickly appeared on my bed along with a knee length black pencil skirt and stilettos with a six-inch heel, I blow out a breath. I've been avoiding Zoltan like Death himself. My mind is still jumbled after I wake curled up like a fetus in front of my bedroom door. A memory of running through the hallways with golden accents, talking to someone about evil spreading through the academy, and Fae feeding magic are like quicksand through my fingers when I try to grasp them. I can't be so messed up from seeing the vampire with another woman that I've lost my mind. Can I? I would've thought that I'm nuts for sure if there isn't one thing still as clear as my own reflection in the mirror in front of me every time I blink.

Snake eyes.

I know they were looking at me from someone else's face as well as I know my own name. Anxiety and excitement churn in my stomach, and I brush my hands over the silky tip again. The red color stands out against my golden skin and blonde hair that's falling around my shoulders every which way. My eyes look too big for my face, red rimmed and still bright from crying. Somehow, my cheeks are also too pale but nothing I can do about it now.

Fenrir came to inform me that the party was starting in an hour, and he left the clothing, letting me know he will be back in precisely thirty minutes to escort me to the formal hall. I did tell him to fuck off and die along with the cursed vampire, or something along those lines, as soon as he mentioned Zoltan. He looked like he wanted to argue, but some morbid satisfaction settled on his face and, nodding primly, he walked away with a bounce in his step.

Maybe insanity follows the Fae genes.

The knock on the door pulls me from my thoughts, and with one last look at the woman in the mirror, I lift my chin up, opening it. Fenrir looks like he is about to faint. Either from the way I'm glaring at him, or because I look like a hot mess.

"Are we going to stand here staring at each other all night, or are we going?" Shouldering my way past the still-gaping Fae, I close and lock the door behind me. "I thought we were not allowed to be late."

"Of course, of course." Stuttering, Fenrir shoves his hand palm up, waiting for me to hand him my key since I don't have a purse.

"Let's go." Slapping the offending thing away, I slip the key to my room in the waistband of my skirt.

Recovering from his ridiculous reaction, Fenrir grabs my elbow and leads me through the hallways. My heels click against the floors, announcing our presence everywhere we turn. Unnerved with the thoughts in my head, the gawking of those we pass makes me more irritated.

"You look nice." Trying to break the charged silence, I glance sideways at Fenrir.

I'm not lying. He does look stunning in his black dress pants and black button-down shirt, the thin golden tie lying flat over his broad chest. His platinum hair is falling like a waterfall over his shoulder and back, two tiny braids bouncing every time his head turns to look at me. In other words, he looks presentable, unlike me. They didn't even give me a bra for fuck's sake. I can feel my breasts bouncing with each step I take.

"Thank you, Hellion." Fenrir stops me from stewing in frustration. "You look stunning."

Snorting, I step awkwardly with my left foot when I try to see if I can feel the blade I strapped on my upper thigh. They may have taken my weapons, but no one said I can't just take one from their wall. I made sure I grabbed the sharpest one I could find. Maybe I'll stab Zoltan with it in the middle of his forehead when I see him. My heart thumps pathetically in my chest. I wish I can rip it out and step on it for being so stupid.

Fenrir's fingers tighten on my elbow. At some point during my time here, I stopped being bothered when he touches me. Not just him, but the jerk vampire, as well. Refusing to consider what that means, I turn to see what the Fae wants.

"Before we get there." He looks conflicted, and I wait, letting him make up his mind. "Before we get there, I think you should know something."

"If you mention Zoltan, I'll have you know that I will take off my shoe and nail you to the wall with it."

"Astara is his sister." Blurting out the words fast, he steps back, releasing my elbow.

If he didn't grab me, I would've ended up on the floor.

176

The weight that was preventing me from filling my lungs with air lifts, my body sagging in Fenrir's hands. My ears are buzzing, lightheadedness forcing my limbs to tremble and cold sweat to bead on my hands and back. Fenrir curses up a storm under his breath as he picks me up, rushing us through the closest open door he can find.

I can't stop shaking.

Words don't want to come, my mouth numbing, and fear spreads through me with the thought that my heart might actually explode. My chest feels tight, and every thump I hear hurts like a knife through my ribs. I'm hyper-ventilating, and all I can do is gasp for air that does not help me breathe. Still cursing, much louder than before, Fenrir shoves my head to my knees, bending me in half, and the strap holding the blade around my thigh cuts into my skin.

"Deep, slow breaths, Francesca." Fenrir's words finally make sense. "Deep, slow breaths. Come now, you will not deprive me of seeing Zoltan grovel at your feet. Would you?"

A hysterical laugh bursts from my lips as my breathing starts slowing down. Tears are sliding down my cheeks and my skirt is soaking them up, so I try to lift my head, but Fenrir presses on it, holding me in place.

"Keep breathing. There we go." Voice soothing, he keeps talking until I finally feel like myself again.

"Let me up, I'm fine." When his hand lingers at the back of my head, reluctant to release me, I honestly laugh. "I promise I'm not going to die on you. I'm fine."

He moves, taking a step back, and I flick my hair away from my face while wiping at my eyes. "I look a mess."

"You look beautiful." He counters without missing a beat.

"And you, my friend, are an excellent liar. Just like any

other Fae I've known." Chuckling, I swipe under my eyes with the tips of my fingers.

"You are half Fae." Pointing an accusing finger at my face, he tries and fails to look stern.

"Touché."

Throwing his head back, his deep musical laughter fills the space around us. The first real smile lifts my lips since I walked into that stupid weapons room. But the reality is a bitch and slaps it off my face with the tick of a second. Groaning, I shove my face in my hands. I don't have to say a word.

Fenrir laughs harder.

"You should've left me to die." My muffled words make him chortle.

"And where would the fun in that be, Hellion." Pulling my hands away, he keeps chuckling. "Come on, this was just a preview of the entertainment for tonight. I'm looking forward to the main act."

"You are a mean asshole, Fenrir." The heat is missing from my voice. "I don't think anyone will miss me if I don't show up."

"I know one someone that will miss you." All the humor leaves his face, and my stomach clenches, dreading his next words. "They are having this gathering in your name. We must show up, Francesca. And you are not to leave my sight. Not even for a second, do you hear me?"

Nodding woodenly, I get off the floor, flattening my skirt and top with my hands. Blowing a deep breath through pursed lips, I steel my resolve. The funny thing is, I'm more nervous about seeing Zoltan than whoever the Board are. It serves me right for acting like a child and running away instead of facing whatever issues I have.

But I'm good at running.

It's all I've been doing my entire life, burying my head in the sand, forcing work or other distractions to fill every moment of my time so I don't have to face life.

Or myself.

"No more running." Glancing at Fenrir, I blow another breath out. "Let's go."

A million scenarios go through my head as Fenrir leads me through the winding hallways and open spaces of the building. Trying to distract myself, I see that not everyone is dressed up and ready for the party. Good thing too, if it means that the entire academy won't see my embarrassment.

The Fae leads me to the back of the building, the walls and floor more elaborately decorated than what I've seen so far. Not wanting to look too interested, I try not to gawk at everything, but there is no doubt in my mind that those are real, precious stones glittering in the candlelight around us. It's like entering a different world, and there is no visible divide separating the two parts of the building.

"It's where only Daywalkers can come. The students are not allowed in this part of the building." Fenrir must've noticed the confusion I feel, explaining it to me without being asked.

"Why? Only your asses can sit on toilets made of gold?" He looks hurt, so I tone down my snarky comments. "Why is there a difference? They risked their lives to be here. Shouldn't you show them why?"

"It is not up to me, Hellion." Steering me towards tall double doors carved with scenes I'm unwilling to look closely at, the Fae shrugs. "I rarely come here myself. It's where the Board resides. I stay with the students."

"Only Daywalkers are allowed, yet here I am being

invited like I'm the queen of the world with a party in my honor."

"A good thing, and we know why." Fenrir stops us at the closed doors. "Just do as we agreed. Stay close to me, and we will be out of here as fast as we can."

Some strange feeling like ghostly fingers shifting through my head makes me stiffen. At first, I think it's a mental attack, something Zoltan was trying to prepare me for before I threw a tantrum and knocked them all unconscious. The energy stays silent, not surging up as it usually did when we practiced my defense against it. It's the only thing stopping me from throwing the double doors open and finding whoever it is that is poking through my head. At a closer inspection, I realize it's not an attack but more a call. A distant buzz announcing its presence like we are old friends.

"Something wrong?" Fenrir steps closer, his body poised for an attack.

Placing my hand on his forearm, I force him to look at me and stop glaring at the empty space around us. A memory of a frail voice telling me stories makes me more confused but brings one thing clear at the front of my mind.

"The archives are in this part of the building." It's not a question, and my words cause Fenrir's eyebrows to almost disappear into his hairline.

"They are."

"Will we be able to go there tonight?"

"We can damn well try, but how did you know?" He is looking down at me, standing so close the scent of forests and rain fills my nostrils.

"Snake eyes." I bite my tongue after blurting those words out. *What the hell is wrong with you, Franky!*

"What?"

"Never mind, I have no idea how I know." Taking a step away from him, I shake my head slightly as if that will clear out my thoughts. "I can feel it, I guess."

Fenrir nods sharply once as if that made all the sense in the world. I'm starting to find it fascinating how he doesn't question me at awkward times when I say things no sane person would. He just takes it in stride as if he hears snake eyes on a daily basis, and like people feeling rooms when they are near them is as normal as saying the moon is up in the sky.

"Ready?" Cocking his arm at me, he waits until I wrap my fingers in the crook of his elbow.

"As ready as I'll ever be." Squaring my shoulders, the fingers from my other hand trace the strap on my thigh through my skirt, giving me extra reassurance. "I can do this."

Fenrir pushes the double doors open.

Chapter Twenty-Four

"I can't do this." My fingers digging into Fenrir's arm will make him bleed soon.

There is no sign of Zoltan, Argoz, or Cassius anywhere. The large room is devoid of furniture, apart from a humongous chandelier that hangs above our heads like an ax in an executioner's hand. The diamonds, because nothing else will produce those rainbows dancing over the floors and people like the precious stones, twinkle at us, reflecting the floating flames—hence the candles.

Magic.

The Board is rubbing it in our faces that they have control over the ancient magic, and there is nothing we can do to stop them. If I wasn't sure that one, or all of them, is our killer, now I am.

And they know we are breathing down their neck.

"Let's keep walking." Fenrir doesn't move his lips as he speaks, a polite smile plastered on his face like a mask.

Shaking off the fear and anger, I follow his lead, but I'm sure I look more constipated than polite. I'm not much of a smiler, you could say. It feels foreign on my face when I'm around people. A glare will look more natural. That thought makes me smile for real.

My feet follow wherever the Fae leads me while I try my best to see everything and everyone without being obvious about it. Faces blend together, and I know I'm making small talk, but I have no idea what I'm saying. Fenrir hasn't stepped on my foot or elbowed me, so I'm guessing the words make sense. I don't know, and I don't care.

A woman steps in my way, and distractedly I smile at her while trying to walk around her. Her cold fingers around my wrist stop me, snapping my eyes to her face. My heart skips a beat when I lock gazes with familiar blue eyes; only these belong to Zoltan's sister. She looks so much like him that I have to be blind not to notice. If only I paid attention the first time I saw her. Embarrassment renders me mute, leaving me to simply stare at her.

"Let me try this the right way." She smiles sheepishly, her cold hand sliding down my wrist and gripping my fingers. "I'm Astara. Zoltan's younger sister."

I want to say it's nice to meet you. "Are there more of you?" Is what comes out of my mouth.

Fenrir snorts, and Astara laughs a beautiful sound that will make a dead man rise from his grave.

"No, it's just, Zoltan and I. No other siblings, unfortunately." she tells Fenrir, her eyes dancing while the smile on her pretty face grows bigger. "I like her."

"As I said you would." The arrogant Fae sniffs primly.

My elbow finds his ribs, and he grunts in pain.

"Scratch that, I absolutely adore her." Astara laughs in Fenrir's scrunched-up-in-pain face.

"Females will be the death of me." Shaking his head, he joins the laughter, and even I giggle a little at that.

"You could've made her blend in better." Astara moves slightly, and I see her blocking the view the rest of the room has of me. "She is standing out like a lamb among the pack of wolves."

The quick glance she sends my camisole makes me look at what she is wearing. A black dress pools down at her feet, the bodice crisscrossed with a golden thread around it that shimmers in the light. Leaning to the side, I look over her shoulder at the rest of the people. Lost in my own thoughts and freaking out because of the reason I am invited here, I don't pay attention at all at to what the others are wearing. Everyone is dressed in black with gold.

Everyone but me.

"Zoltan is going to flip." Astara looks at Fenrir pointedly.

"I can't wait." Grinning like a fool, he gets another elbow in his ribs.

"My life is not a joke!" Hissing at him, I yank my hand away from his arm. "If I live long enough, I'm going to make you pay for this, you jerk."

"We know why they want you here, Francesca. They know that we know why they want you here. This"— Waving his hand at my clothing, he makes sure my gaze is locked on his before he continues— "tells them to go fuck themselves. We, more importantly, *you*, are not afraid."

"He does make a good point," Astara says without turning, so my glare gets wasted on her back.

"I thought I liked you, too. I changed my mind." Clenching my fists when she laughs, I sweep the room again with my eyes. "Where the hell are the others?"

"That's what I'd like to know." Fenrir is looking around as well. "The Board is not here either."

"My brother should've been one of the first to arrive.

He rushed out of his room, hoping to catch Francesca as she enters the hall."

"So, where is he?" My teeth are making a great work on the inside of my mouth. If I keep it up, I might just chew through it and make the ghoul proud.

"Let's do another round." Fenrir snatches my hand without waiting on an answer, dragging me along with him. Astara trails only a step behind us.

Catching myself twice when my smile slips, I give up after the third when another guy stops our progress, droning on about some project he's been working on. When Astara yanks me back by the waistband of my skirt, I'm horrified to see I've stepped in the guy's face, and my fangs are digging on the inside of my lower lip. With a tight-lipped smile, I turn away, my eyes widening when they meet Astara's.

"We will be right back."

Pulling me away from Fenrir, Zoltan's sister leads me away until we find a secluded spot between two large windows. The soft glow of the floating flames does not reach this area, leaving it cast in shadows. My shoulders sag when we stop, and I'm glad to see I'm not the only one. All the pretense disappears from Astara's face, and she leans on the wall next to me.

"I don't like this." When her head rolls on her shoulders so she can see me, my feelings are reflected in the distressed look on her face. "Something is not right."

Mind spinning, I try and fail to come up with an idea of what to do.

"Can we go look for him?"

"I can…" Astara pales, sucking in a sharp breath.

My head turns slowly, dread like lead settling in the pit of my stomach. My heart lodges in my throat when I see two demon guards dragging Zoltan to the center of the hall. Outraged cries, gasps and shouts bounce off the walls around me but I can't look away from the vampire. His head is hanging to his chest, rolling limply on his shoulders, and his feet are dragging on the floor. My feet move so I can get my hands on the two demons that dare touch him, but Astara pulls me back so harshly I hear the thread ripping in the seams of my top.

"Don't you dare move; he will kill me if I let anything happen to you." Snapping at me, her hand tightens on my clothes.

"He will be dead if we don't do something, Astara. I doubt he can come back from that just to kill you."

"You obviously don't know my brother that well." But her lips are pressed in a white line, and I can tell she wants to rush to him as bad as I want to.

"Where the fuck is Fenrir?"

My whole body is tingling, the energy twisting and turning like a tornado waiting to be unleashed. My skin feels too tight, and I know I'm going to go supernova soon if I don't find a target for it. That's when I see the Fae skirting the crowd that has formed a circle around the two demons and Zoltan. They drop him like dead weight on the marbled floor.

Nudging Astara, I jerk my chin to point at Fenrir. We both stand coiled up, ready to spring if the demons try to do anything to Zoltan while he is out for the count. My gaze finds him again, his black hair tousled, and his shirt ripped in a few places. A red haze bathes the room around me when I see blood pooling under his body.

"He is alive." Astara must've noticed the same thing because her cold fingers find my forearm, her nails digging into my skin. "Listen, you can hear his heartbeat. He is still alive."

Looking away from him, I concentrate on his heartbeat while trying to see Fenrir again. The Fae is nowhere to be found, so I keep looking until the crowd starts parting, getting my full attention. That same guy with the project that pissed me off earlier walks up to stand in front of the three newcomers with arms crossed over his chest.

"What is the meaning of this?" His voice booms like a cannon in the silent room.

The three men that just entered the room stand shoulder to shoulder as they face the project guy. I don't remember his name, and I feel bad for wanting to rip him apart earlier. I might apologize later if I survive this. The robes covering the three new men are enough to tell me who they are.

The Board.

The one on the far left with his dark hair and soulless black eyes is unmistakably a vampire. Not because of his features or the alluring power rolling off him in waves. The most prominent fangs I've ever seen, as thick and as long as my pinky, are a dead giveaway. His lips, pulled back in a snarl while he watches project guy, are as red as my top.

The man in the middle is the shortest in height out of the three, but his body is bulkier, his robe stretching within an inch of its life over his shoulders. Dirty blond hair sticks all over the place atop of his head, the thick sideburns connecting it to the short beard covering the lower part of his square face. A flat nose, as if it's been broken way too many times to count and can't heal properly, sits between two yellow eyes, marking him as a shifter. A feline of some sort if I'm not mistaken.

The third is the most unassuming one. Rail thin, with a hookish nose and long, limp, pepper-colored hair. He looks like the meanest of them all. A mage if I have to place a bet. His light green eyes flick from one face to the next, ignoring project guy like he is not even standing there. His twitching fingers get my attention off his cold, emotionless face, and my chest tightens when sparks fly from their tips and electricity flickers between them. Now I know why Zoltan is unconscious. My whole being centers on the Mage.

"That fucker is mine," I tell Astara in case she noticed the same thing, but she doesn't answer. I can't look away from the Mage to see what she is doing.

"He broke the rules." The shifter speaks with a growl as if his animal is too close under his skin.

"What rules can Zoltan break? He is the one enforcing them on all of us." Project guy does not back off, my respect for him growing.

"He contacted an outsider in hopes of bringing him on our land." The vampire spits the words like they taste vile on his tongue.

"Lie! He does not like outsiders, everyone knows this." Project guy looks around at the gathered people like he expects support, but everyone stares mutely at him. With a frown, he turns back at the three men. "Who was he contacting?"

"He had an arranged meeting with Roberti." My heart stops for the tenth time this night. They couldn't possibly kill Roberti, could they? And what the hell was Zoltan thinking to contact my boss without telling me about it?

Project guy laughs.

My jaw hangs open at the audacity of this guy. Who the hell is he? Can I count on him when shit hits the fan, or will he side with the rest of them? And where on earth is Fenrir?

"You are getting bored without going out in the field for too long. Or whoever is whispering in your ear is feeding you horse shit." Project guy does not back down.

The Mage nods at someone on the side, and I hold my breath, expecting Fenrir to be the next to be dragged in front of everyone. But it's not, although that would've been a better option. Andrius Roberti strides through the crowd like he owns the place. I stare stupidly at him, not understanding what is going on. Is he taking over the academy? Can he even do that? And if he can, why the fuck did he send me here in the first place?

"No one whispers in their ear. They saw it with their own eyes." Roberti speaks, and something inside me dies.

He knew.

Andrius knew all along that the killer was looking for me, and he sent me here for that reason alone. Not because he cared about the killed residents that counted on his protection.

"Where is Francesca hiding?" His question snaps my eyes to his face, and our gazes lock across the vast space.

Chapter Twenty-Five

Everything I've ever felt disappears from me. I feel like a stranger in my own skin as my feet move on their own despite Astara trying to hold me back. Conversations fleet through my mind, Roberti's words that he wants to figure me out the loudest among them. My boss has always played the long game. While the rest of us stare at the trees, he sees the forest.

Has he been planning this very moment since the day he found me covered in blood?

I have no doubt in my mind that he has.

But it's no longer just about me now, is it?

His chocolate eyes track my movement, the same ones that used to give me courage now feeding me dread. Just the sound of my stilettos clicking at an even rhythm on the marble disturbs the quiet blanketing the room. No one is even breathing, their attention centered on me. Astara had it right from the start.

A lamb amid a pack of wolves.

What they don't know is that this lamb has teeth. And it bites back.

My feet falter when Fenrir stumbles into the cleared-up space, his hair falling over his face before he yanks it away angrily, glaring over his shoulder. Following the direction of his gaze, I can't even feel the shock that's trying to stun me when Cassius glares back a moment before he walks up and shoves the Fae closer to Zoltan's unconscious form.

"You snake!" Astara hisses from behind me. She must've followed when she couldn't stop me from walking out of the shadows. "My brother trusted you, you pathetic excuse for a life."

"My daughter trusts me as well." The mammoth of a man lifts his chin up unapologetically.

"And you think they give a shit about you or that little brat? Not even you can be that stupid." Astara is getting louder with each word spoken, and I tune her out, focusing entirely on Roberti.

The demigod's gaze sweeps me from head to toe, and revulsion brings bile up the back of my throat. I trusted him. I fed from him. His blood is inside my body, and it's burning like acid through my veins right now. He must've seen it written all over my face.

"Don't look so hurt now, Drake." His hand lifts towards my face, and I take a step back. He mistakes it for fear and smirks. "This is nothing personal."

"Of course not." My voice sounds flat and devoid of emotion. The blade burns a hole on the inside of my thigh, my fingers itching to grab it.

"If you are to execute one of us, it must be with the agreement of the entire Board." Project guy finds his voice again.

I admire the man at this point.

"Very well." The vampire from the Board looks pointedly at the demon guards, and they spring into action, bolting out of the hall.

"Was Aiden in on it, too?" I'm not sure why I ask, but since we are obviously waiting for something to happen, it'll at least fill the time.

"That idiot is in love with you. I almost had to kill him to stop him from coming after you here, messing up all my plans." Roberti looks disgusted as he spits the words.

How have I not seen this side of him?

You didn't want to see it. That snarky voice in my head has perfect timing, as always.

Awareness spreads through me like a physical touch. I will recognize it if I am dead and six feet under the ground. My heart does a painful thump, and I open to it, letting it sink inside me, as desperate for it as my lungs are for air. It's all that I needed to allow the energy churning in my chest free reign. Roberti's patronizing smirk slips from his arrogant face while my smile grows. My heartbeat slows down, the calmness blanketing my insides.

"What I find funny in all this"—Kicking off the damn stilettos that have been killing my feet for hours, I roll my head on my shoulders— "is that you thought you would win."

Thump.

Throwing myself at Roberti, I send us both rolling on the marble floors. My fists beat a staccato rhythm as they jab his ribs until he lodges a knee between us, kicking me away. I keep rolling until I end up in a crouch, the sound of the skirt ripping down the sides too loud to my ears. My gaze locks with Roberti's panicked one. I guess he didn't get the chance to hear about all the little tricks a half blood can do.

Thump.

Power slams me when he unleashes his full strength, which would've doubled me over a week ago. Thanks to Zoltan, this is a child's play right now and my grin grows when Roberti takes a step back. Releasing the hold on the torrent in my chest, I feel the blast that gushes out of me, lifting the demigod in the air. He gawks, his eyes widening for a moment as he floats, suspended in the air, before being thrown away like a dirty sock across the hall. The building shudders from the impact.

Thump.

"She is my sister." Zoltan's deep voice makes me turn to look at him. My knees almost buckle seeing him animated and standing. I watch him move, every punch and kick like a beautiful dance as he sends man after man tumbling through the space. Bones crunch, breaking with each contact he makes. His eyes are glowing, the fangs poking under his full upper lip, and I watch him mesmerized.

"She is my sister." Repeating the words, he sends a quick glance to make sure I'm paying attention.

"I know."

A woman with more massive biceps than my thighs sneaks up at his back. I spring into action, my foot connecting with her face in a round kick that sends her crashing at three others behind her. My back connects with Zoltan's as we watch those siding with the Board and Roberti circling us.

"I should've told you." He doesn't sound happy, and I chuckle.

Thump.

My back bows, dropping me to my knees when a current of power enters my every pore. Zoltan roars, but I'm already moving. Wrapping my fingers on his shoulders, I use him as a bouncing board, sending my body up in the air, and I land with my knees on Cassius's chest. We both go down, and I ride him like a slide to the floor. Tucking my head down, I roll away from him, pulling out the blade at the same time.

Zoltan does not allow me to have fun. He barrels into Cassius like a truck, tucking his shoulder at the larger man's gut. I leave them to it, searching for Roberti or the Board. The three men are nowhere to be found. Roberti is missing as well. Craning my neck, I finally spot the Board members close to the large double doors of the hall, and I spring at them, jumping over bodies and spinning around fighting men.

Thump.

The vampire is the first to see me coming, both his hands lifting in the air. Dropping to my knees, I slide at him, avoiding whatever blast he sent my way and taking him down when I collide with his feet. My hand lifts in the air, fingers gripping the blade so tight there will be an imprint of the hilt on the skin of my palm. The soulless black eyes on his face widen, horror written all over his arrogant features when he sees his end a breath away.

"Stop!" Nothing could've stopped my hand but the frail voice and softly spoken demand.

Everyone stops, and you can hear a pin drop while the two demon guards carry a platform with a sleeping man on it. A memory nudges at the back of my mind, but I'm too stunned that the voice pulled me out of the trance to care about it. Even the three assholes from the Board are watching the newcomer with respect, reverence and fear.

"Did we start killing each other in our home now?" The frail voice asks, and I see the sleeping guy's lips moving, but his eyes stay closed.

"No Soren, we have an intruder that has entered our grounds." The shifter growls, his hate-filled glare aimed right at me.

I grin at him.

I can't explain why, but the presence of this person brings me confidence and peace. I should really be worried because tonight is evidence enough that I'm stupidly trusting the wrong people.

"An intruder passing the trials." The guy, Soren, doesn't sound convinced. "I need to see him."

"It's a girl," the Mage from the Board says in disgust, and Zoltan saddles next to me, yanking me behind his back.

"A girl passes the trials. The rest of you decide to kill her, while one of our strongest is standing as a shield in front of her as we speak." Soren chuckles, "And you call her an intruder."

Zoltan stiffens, and even Fenrir and Astara block me from the sides like a living shield, just like Soren said, but he still has his eyes closed. As if this night is not weird enough.

"Step away, Zoltan. I mean her no harm." Soren chuckles again when Zoltan growls low in his throat. 'Come closer child, I wish to see you."

Placing my palms flat on Zoltan's back, I try to push him away, but he is an unmovable rock in front of me. Unless we are planning on fighting our way out of here, I need to go and see what Soren wants. The feeling that he will not hurt me sits at the forefront of my mind. Since I can't move the stubborn vampire, I shoulder Fenrir away and stride purposely towards Soren.

"Francesca, get back here." Zoltan's hiss stops me for a second, but I continue moving.

"Intruder, she is not," Soren says when my feet bring me next to him. The demon guards watch the blade I'm still clutching in my hand warily.

"She is not a Daywalker, nor can she become one," the Mage snaps angrily. "She is a half blood."

"A half-blood walking our grounds for a week until you decided she is not worthy of gracing us with her presence." Soren's head turns to the side, his eyes still closed. "Were you not aware she was here?"

"We were tricked to believe that she is a pure-blooded Fae, a mate to Fenrir," the shifter grumbles.

"And you think we should kill her."

"The rules have been followed since the foundations of this institution were set." The Mage looks like he expects applause.

"Truth." Soren's voice cracks, and I grip the blade tighter. "And do the rules say we kill one of our own?"

"Of course not! Not unless they break their oath." The Mage flicks his light green eyes at the other two robed men.

"Not even the students in this academy." Soren waits for confirmation, and after nodding like an idiot, the Mage realizes he can't be seen.

"Not even the students," he says a little louder.

"Let me see that blade, child." It takes a second to understand he addressed me.

Without thinking, I shove the dagger in his face, making everyone hiss a warning. My lips twist in a grimace, and I ignore them. The guy asked, so it's not like I stabbed him. Warm, thin fingers wrap over my own. I watch it like it's happening to someone else when Soren's hand moves fast, pulling the blade from my hand and slashing both our palms at the same time. Shouts create chaos around us, an unfamiliar power blanketing me. Panic stops the breath in my throat when I feel my blood pulling back up my veins instead of flowing like it normally does. Understanding dawns on me that whoever it is, they are trying to stop me from bleeding out of the open wound on my hand. Looking over my shoulder, I see Zoltan, his eyes locked on my palm and glowing brighter than ever before. I've never felt his powers like this. Almost as if they belong to somebody else.

My brain kicks into gear, realizing how bad all this must be if he will rather stop my heart than allow my blood to leave my body. I want to squeeze my hand so I can help him out, but I can't move. My heart is barely beating in my chest, and terror numbs me as I watch one drop separate from my skin and fall into Soren's open hand, splattering over his pale skin.

A foreign energy, ancient magic, the primal sense of something larger and more powerful than life itself spreads through me, overwhelming my senses, and all sound comes back in a rush.

"She is not an intruder." Soren's voice sounds intense, and it quiets everyone. "She is just like me." His snake eyes open, locking on mine. "She is dragon blood."

I feel Zoltan at my back, his arms wrapping around me and holding me upright. Memories assault my brain of the night before when I found the sleeping Fae. The promises he made me make. The oath he forced from me. Soren is smiling like he just won an award, but I have a horrible feeling that it was a death sentence for me. When Fenrir steps next to us, his hand gripping my shoulder in silent support, I know I am right.

"Welcome to Daywalker Academy, Francesca Drake. Your training and education will begin immediately."

"Soren, what did you do?" The fear in Zoltan's voice makes dark spots dance at the corners of my eyes.

"I tied her life to mine." Soren smiles brighter. "And mine is tied to all of yours. If you kill her, you will all die."

"Well, fuck." My words are slurred, and I finally succumb to the darkness.

Next in the Daywalker Series

vinci-books.com/infiltrated

Welcome to Daywalker Academy—where love is lethal and secrets kill.

My mission's gone sideways, and now I'm bound to the Academy —and to a vampire I should never want. The city's on the edge of war.

And I'm falling for the one who could burn it all down.

Turn the page for a free preview…

Infiltrated: Chapter One

The night is beautiful.

There is something calming and reassuring when I am surrounded by shadows, the silvery light of the moon shining down but only occasionally caressing me like gentle fingers. The silence is full of mystery and life if you pay close attention to it.

It speaks.

Tightening my arms around my bent knees, pressing my chin on them, I watch the treetops sway in the forest encircling us. The pregnant moon hangs low in the sky, bathing everything in an enchanted glow like a cloud of glittery dust sprinkled everywhere. It would be serene and dreamlike if we are not talking about nightmares. Red and yellow eyes pop up here and there, shifters and demons patrolling the grounds and destroying the illusion by bringing reality into play—a not so subtle reminder that our lives are in their hands. Well, not my life, but everyone else's.

One might think this is a prison, not an academy.

The longer I sit on the windowsill, my spine rubbing on

the harsh stone at my back, the later in the night it gets. The temperatures are dropping, condensing the glass and blurring my view. Everything seems to move further away, my turbulent thoughts fighting for attention in hopes of dragging me down the slippery slope of despair. I don't want to be here, but I can't leave.

I tried.

The moment I came around after losing consciousness at the declaration Soren made, I pushed everyone away from me and bolted out of the building. His words followed me like a curse echoing inside my head. *"I tied her life to mine. And mine is tied to all of yours. If you kill her, you will all die."* That wouldn't have been that bad if he didn't hit me with, *"Welcome to Daywalker Academy, Francesca Drake. Your training and education will begin immediately,"* right before it.

So I ran.

My feet barely touched the ground as I fled through the forest, low branches and tall shrubs snagging my skin and clothing as if they wanted to hold me back. I still remember the stinging pain like thousands of papercuts across my skin as my hair streamed behind me, my breaths sharp in my ears. And all that for nothing. The moment I neared the gate, all my strength left me and I crumpled on the forest floor like a marionette with cut-off strings. I can still smell the scent of wilting and decaying leaves and wet soil, as well as the stench of blood soaking the earth under my nose when the skin on my face was pressed on the ground by an invisible force holding me down.

I've never felt so powerless and weak.

The skin on my arms pebbles with the memory of that night a week ago. Zoltan's arms wrapping around me and lifting me to his chest is the only pleasant memory, and it only makes me angrier. All of them play gods with my life one way or another, regardless of the motivation behind it. Zoltan, Fenrir, Roberti, Soren…every single one of them think they have a right to make decisions in my name.

A weight settles on my shoulders, pressing me down. I know I shouldn't let the thoughts depress me, or I might as well kill myself now. Feeling sorry for myself is not going to get me out of this shitstorm. The more I think about it that way, the less depressed I feel. I can always depend on myself to get out of whatever crap I've gotten myself into. It may not be stealthy or smooth, but it can be done. If there is a body count and blood trail left behind, so be it.

A grin lifts the corners of my mouth.

"You see, that." From the corner of my eye, Fenrir waves an accusing finger at my face. "That look on your face right there…it tells me trouble is coming. Whatever you are thinking, you should stop now."

The damn Fae is like a bad smell. I can't get rid of him no matter how hard I try. Wherever I turn, I see him watching me warily, as if he expects me to grow horns or something. Always watching. Always only a few feet away.

Annoying as fuck!

Dread and fear have me in their clutches, their claws embedding deeply into my very soul. But I'll never let any of them see how desperate I am to turn back time and never return home the night I found Roberti waiting for me in my apartment. *Never let them see your fear, Franky.* Reminding myself of that, I allow my grin to grow.

"I don't like it," Fenrir grumbles while I do my best to ignore him.

Huffing, he folds his arms across his chest, eyes narrowed on me like he thinks he can read my mind. Standing in the same spot for the last few hours, he is leaning on the wall next to the window, head tilted to the side so he can look at my face. In the darkened hallway, if it wasn't for his platinum hair neatly tied at the base of his neck and the golden glow of his skin, he would blend in with the shadows wearing his long-sleeved black shirt and black pants. The golden emblem—a dragon sitting on top of his left pectoral—is like a hot poker in my eye. I hate it as much as I hate Roberti right now.

"You can't ignore me forever."

"I can try." Finally giving in, I pull my gaze from the misty window and lock it on his. "Anyone told you that you are as annoying as a mosquito on a hot summer night?"

"I'll have you know that females have never complained about my company." If possible, his eyes narrow further, turning into slits.

"I'm pretty sure none of them had their life ripped from their hands at the time, either." Okay, so it is a shitty thing to say, but it's not like he didn't ask for it.

Flinching like I just physically slapped him, the Fae drops all pretense, his face softening and shoulders slumping in defeat. My own stiffen, knowing what's coming next.

"Francesca, no matter what I say and how many times I apologize, I can't change anything that has already happened." With a sigh, he rubs his fingers over his forehead. "We screwed up. All of us. No one expected for any of this to happen."

"I don't want to talk…"

"And instead of pushing all of us away"—He continues talking like I haven't said a word—"you need to stop for a moment to hear us out. We can't change the situation, but we can turn it to our advantage."

Pressing my lips in a firm line, mostly to keep my mouth shut more than anything else, I glare at him. As if that is me encouraging him, he gets animated, pushing off the wall to face me better, his arms waving around with each word. The silver light of the moon washes over his face, giving him an ethereal look too perfect to be mistaken for anything else but an immortal.

"Think about it." Reaching for my arm, my scowl deepens, and Fenrir stops an inch before making contact. "As bad as it looks, they played with open cards thinking they had all of us cornered. No one expected Soren to even stir, much less speak. It gave us the upper hand, and now we know who's behind some of the problems we are facing. Would you rather run, or would you rather take advantage of it, destroy them, and stop whatever it is they are planning on doing?" Dropping his arm limply to his side, his fist clenches and a muscle ticks in his jaw. "Intentionally or not, Soren gave you an opening you can't just throw away. For all our sakes, you must see this for the opportunity what it is."

"Don't you dare lecture me, Fae!" Hissing, I bare my fangs at him, forcing him to take a step back. His eyes widen comically, and I realize I've moved, poised on the windowsill on my hands and knees ready to pounce on him. "Who should I look for that is planning something? You? Zoltan, Roberti, the Board, Soren…? There are too many of you and only one of me. What would you have me do?"

I know that I'm not fair to him, or Zoltan for that matter. They did prove whose side they were on the day my life went to shit…well the day my life got more screwed up than it already was anyway. But I can't help being defensive and bitter.

They all lied.

"You need to let him talk to you." Shaking off the initial reaction to my aggression, Fenrir squares his shoulders.

And there it is.

The reason the Fae follows me around like a lost puppy through the floors and hallways.

Zoltan.

An unfortunate-for-him side effect of having his blood in my veins is that I can feel the vampire whenever he gets near me. Not a few feet or anything. I can feel him from a few yards away, thankfully. It helps avoid crossing paths with him, even if it makes me look insane when people see me fleeing through the building like it's on fire. Knowing that he can't come in the hallway leading to Soren's room is a perk I take advantage of all the time. I don't know the reason why he can't cross whatever invisible barrier exists, but I don't question it. Maybe the old-as-dirt Soren has a twisted sense of humor and loves torturing Zoltan. I wouldn't put it past him.

"I have nothing to say, Fenrir." With a sigh, I settle back down on the windowsill, the scraping of fabric against wood filling up the quiet space around us when I shift my legs to curl them under me. "I still haven't processed everything. Until a day ago, all I was capable of doing was screaming 'oh shit' in my head. I'm sure even an old fart like yourself can understand that." Smirking at his glare, I lean my head back, looking at him through half-closed lids. "I need time."

"We don't have time." Pushing the words through clenched teeth, the Fae looks ready to drag me kicking and screaming to do what he wants me to do.

"Says the immortal." I can't help it when the corners of my lips tilt up at his pissed-off face.

"Long-lived and immortal are two different things. Not all of us have eternity." His mouth snaps shut audibly, and I see his breath gets caught as soon as the words are out of his mouth.

"What does that mean?" He got my full attention with

his slip up, my heartbeat speeding up at the implications of it. "You're not planning on dying, are you?"

"You won't get rid of me that easily, I assure you." Fenrir winks, but I notice his fists clenching when he thinks I can't see it.

"I know I'm not that lucky. You and that damn vampire are like a curse I'll never be rid of." There is no fire in my comment, yet Fenrir stiffens regardless. I watch him for a long moment before deciding to drop it and let him be for now. Judging by the way we are looking at each other, neither one of us is in the mood to go down that rocky road.

Glancing down the empty hallway as if expecting some-one, Fenrir locks gazes with me before breathing out a deep sigh. "I have a class to teach."

"Hurry along then." Flicking my fingers in a shooing motion, I grin at his frown. "Go annoy someone else. I could use five minutes of peace."

"Please don't get in trouble while I'm gone." Looking down his nose at me, he transforms in front of my eyes. From Fenrir, the guy following at my heels, to the royal Fae that expects all of us to bow at his feet. "I'll find you when I'm done."

With that, he spins on his heel and saunters down the hallway, leaving the scent of forests and rain in his wake. I watch him walk away, his broad shoulders swinging with each firm step he takes, his clothing molding to his body like a second skin. Thanks to a certain vampire, it does nothing for me, but it still should be illegal for any man to look the way Fenrir does. Good thing they keep him here away from human women. Can a female go insane from seeing perfec-tion? I hope we never have to find out.

"You can come out now." Still looking in the direction

Fenrir disappeared, I blow out a slow breath. "He won't be back for at least an hour."

"You knew I was here." Astara comes out of the shadows as if she's stepping through a portal from another realm. "How? Not even the Fae was aware of my presence."

Shrugging a shoulder, I turn to look out the window, my eyes following a drop of condensation trickling down the glass. "I don't know…" my voice trails off, and Astara slides on the windowsill opposite me, curling her legs underneath her just as I have mine, our knees touching slightly.

"You want to talk about it?" Her voice is soft, and I see from the corner of my eye that she's looking out the window too, her hair falling over her shoulder covering most of her face.

"No."

"You want me to leave?" Her body shifts slightly, telling me that if I say yes, she will honor my wishes and disappear as fast as she appeared at my side.

"No."

"Okay." Leaning her head on the wall behind her, she gets more comfortable. "If we get interrupted in pretending we don't see each other, I got it. I'll rip their throat out."

"You're angry?" Feeling bad that I've ignored her for no other reason than the fact that she is related to Zoltan, I almost continue talking, but her laughter snaps my mouth shut.

"Angry?" Still chuckling, Astara bumps her knee to mine in a weird nudge. "No, I'm just hungry."

A burst of laughter comes from me, echoing and bouncing off the walls around us. Shaking my head, I finally relax my shoulders, the tense muscles of my back loosening the knots that were giving me a headache. Leave it to a vampire to disperse tension by mentioning violence.

Infiltrated: Chapter Two

My fists clench when I push my hands further into the pockets of my pants. Pressing my elbows close to my sides so I can avoid any contact, I wade through the throng of people rushing to get to wherever their next class should be.

Studying is the last thing on my mind.

After Soren's declaration that I'm a student here, clothing magically appears in my room, filling up a closet the size of my apartment back in Sienna. Mostly the same black ensemble everyone else is wearing, but there are a few colorful pieces that scream Fenrir from a mile away. The Fae thinks he is sneaky as shit, but I'm onto him and his antics.

Not that I'll tell him that.

Also, every second day, there is a cup of fresh blood waiting for me, one I'm yet to summon enough self-control to refuse. I can smell Zoltan's essence in it as soon as I open my eyes, making my mouth water and fangs descend until they are throbbing in my gums. Like a feral animal in bloodlust, I attack it each time, slurping and licking the walls of the glass. It should be freaky knowing he can enter my room even though the door is always locked while I sleep, but surprisingly it doesn't bother me as much as it should.

I won't tell the damn vampire that I'm onto him, either.

Astara, on the other hand, just hangs around me the second I'm alone, not saying a word. Apparently, it's our thing now, sitting next to each other in utter silence. It's strangely comforting, so I welcome it. I did tell her as much before resuming our mute get-togethers.

"Which class?" A familiar male voice pulls me from my thoughts, my head snapping sharply in his direction. Jerking back, he lifts both hands palms up in surrender, but a huge grin blossoms on his face. "Just asking because it seems we are going in the same direction."

I narrow my eyes at the wolf shifter I had the unfortunate pleasure of meeting at the gates when I took on the stupid mission that got me in this mess. His hair flops messily over his high forehead, almost dropping over his yellow eyes. I can see his animal lurking in the depth of his gaze, as if it doesn't want to miss anything. The prickly shadow that seems permanent over his square jaw gives him a roguish appearance.

We tried to kill each other then.

Nothing has changed now. I still want to kill him, despite his handsome face.

"Half of these people are walking in the same direction." Grinding my teeth, I turn away, staring ahead at nothing in particular. "Go away."

"I think we started off on the wrong foot." Undeterred, he falls in step with me, even when I try my best to leave him behind by walking as fast as I can without running. "I was only doing my job."

"This matters to me why?" Dodging people left and right, I tangle my fingers in the fabric of my pants so I don't wrap them around his neck. "I'm not here to make friends. Go away!"

"Listen." Keeping his voice conversational as if I haven't spoken, he glances quickly around us to see if anyone is paying attention before moving slightly closer to me. "Guards, and those like me, hear lots of things…" his voice trails off when we pass a couple of demons, their red eyes zeroed in on me burning with hatred. I grin widely at them, loving the glares I receive in return. "Things you might want to know in case someone, let's say, tries to set a trap for you."

The wolf gets all my attention, my shoulders stiffening at the warning in his words. My feet slow down, and my head swivels to look at him. Like he hasn't said a word, he looks ahead, walking unassumingly by my side. Nothing to see here, folks. He just threatened a half blood.

"You need to work on your threats, pup." I surprise myself with the malice in my softly spoken words. "Bigger and badder things have tried to kill me, yet here I am, dealing with a fleabag like yourself."

"You misunderstood me, Francesca." I can tell I pissed him off, but I must give him credit for not snarling like I can tell he really wants to. "It wasn't a threat; it was a warning."

"What? We are friends now, and you give a shit what happens to me?" Chuckling humorlessly, I resume walking, leaving him lagging for a few moments.

"You are the one acting like a pup." He catches up quickly. "Reacting on instinct and lashing out when you are cornered." I can see him shaking his head as if disappointed. "I expected more from you."

"You don't even know me." Cringing at the defensiveness in my tone, I bump into the person walking by me, causing her to take a step back as she stumbles out of the way. "Sorry..." murmuring under my breath, I tighten my elbows even closer, almost causing pain in my back.

"True," my new buddy chirps from next to me. "But I do hear things, as I said. I've heard a lot about Agent Drake from those in Sienna. What I see now..." his voice trails off, and he gets the reaction he was hoping for.

I give him an expectant look, and that stupid smile makes an appearance again. "Well?" Growling the question, I hate that I ask but am completely unable to stop myself.

"I see a wounded pup." Going back to the analogy I used on him, his smile grows at my scowl. "Unlike the fierce and formidable female that most of Sienna are wary of. You should be picking your allies and forming a plan. Instead, you are trying to bite the hands that are reaching out to help you. Not a smart move." His head bobs up and down like he agrees with his own statement. "Not smart at all."

We are passing one of the giant stairways leading to the second floor, and I use it to my advantage. Grabbing the shifter by the arm, I yank him under it, slamming his back on the wall as I get in his face, teeth bared in a snarl. His fingers wrap in a punishing grip over my upper arms, his nails digging in my skin.

"Listen to me, wolf." Our faces are so close that if anyone sees us, they'll think we are about to kiss with our noses almost touching. "I don't need your help or any information you want to share. I'll say this only once. Stay away from me if you want to keep breathing."

His fingers tighten and the wolf comes closer to the surface, searching my face through his eyes. I can feel the sharp points of his claws poking holes in my shirt as he wrestles with his animal to keep it in check. If I want to call myself smart—even though most already know I'm not—I shouldn't have done what I did. Aggressively manhandling a shifter is not what you do, not unless you want them to tear your throat out. He might have a point that I'm lashing out with no reason, but that's beside the point. It's how I deal with things out of my control.

"What are you afraid of, Francesca Drake?" His deep voice rumbles, vibrating through his chest into mine where we are pressed close together.

"I fear nothing, you fool." Pushing off of him, I whirl around to leave, but he jerks me back, still holding onto my arms.

"That is not true." Those yellow eyes are too knowing, causing my spine to stiffen. "You fear yourself." The shifter's head tilts to the side, sending a sharp ping through my chest. "Well, what do you know. You are a lot smarter than I gave you credit for."

"Remove your hands." Pushing the words through clenched teeth, I feel that telltale sign of calm loosening my muscles and slowing down my heart.

Whatever it is that the shifter sees in my face widens his eyes, and he drops his hands like I burnt him. His reaction snaps me out of the trancelike state that almost pulled me under, forcing me to suck in harsh breaths through my nose.

"Don't touch me, wolf." My throat feels rough when I speak, and I swallow in hopes to moisten the dryness. "Instead of wondering if I'm smart, you should think about your own actions." Turning away, I stop right before coming out from under the stairway. "They can get you killed really fast."

Leaving the shifter behind, I join the throng of people, blending in with the sea of bodies moving through the halls. His gaze follows me for a long time, the feeling of being watched raising the short hairs on the back of my neck. I'm not surprised when Astara joins me, falling seamlessly into step with me a minute later.

"Problem?" she asks casually, as if we've been having a conversation for a while.

"For his sake, I hope not." The jackhammering of my heart that she can no doubt hear clearly calls me a liar. Wisely, Astara doesn't mention that little fact. Neither do I.

"Listen," she says reluctantly, and I turn to look at her when she pauses for too long. "I know we have our thing going on here…"

"You mean hanging out while pretending we don't see that the other is around?" She snorts ungracefully at that, and I chuckle.

"Yeah, that thing," she mumbles.

A guy I've never seen before blocks our path, and I stop along with her. With an athletic build and as tall as she is, his pale skin and phantom-less eyes tell me he is a vampire. A scar runs from his eyebrow and disappears in his chestnut hair, which pulls my eyebrows in a frown. Supernaturals don't scar. What could possibly have left a mark on his face? I don't get a chance to study him long or ask about it. Astara lifts her hand, fingers outstretched like claws, and wraps them over his face, the blood-red color of her long nails standing out against his skin. Not missing a beat, she moves him to the side, shoving his head none too gently the moment he is out of her way, then she continues walking as if nothing happened. I gape at his pissed off face before rushing to catch up with her.

"But I feel like I should say something about Leo," Astara continues our conversation.

"Who?" Still giving the vampire glances over my

shoulder while he stares daggers at our backs, I almost miss what she says next.

"The werewolf you were snuggling with." Her long, graceful fingers flick in the direction of the tall, winding stairway.

"No, I mean who is Leo…" When what she said registers, I snatch her by the arm, yanking her to a stop. "Wait, what?"

"The shifter…" she says it very slowly like she's talking to a simpleton, her eyes boring into mine as if she is trying to see if I'm all there.

"I wasn't snuggling with him." Glaring at her, I debate if I should punch her when she throws her head back and laughs in my face.

"It sure looked like you were, and someone didn't get the memo before running off to tell my brother." Her smile grows impossibly wide like the cat who ate the canary. "Oh look, Fenrir looks like someone spit in his coffee, too." Giggling, she points over my shoulder.

With dread building in my stomach, I turn very slowly to see what she's looking at. The number of people mulling the halls is significantly less now, and it's easy to see Zoltan and Fenrir marching towards the wolf like some choreographed strategic attack, hoarding him from both sides. The shifter stands unfazed, watching them getting near. He is much braver than I am. If I see those two with murderous looks on their faces like they have now, I'd be bolting out of here so fast that only clouds of dust will be left in my wake. When the wolf turns to look at us over his shoulder, he smiles and winks, and I decide right there that he is actually insane.

My feet move to stop the idiots from killing the poor

guy, but Astara jerks me back by grabbing a fistful of my shirt. "Let them be."

"They'll kill him. Look at them." When she lifts one perfect eyebrow at my comment, I shake my head. "If anyone is going to kill the asshole, it'll be me. I don't need bodyguards."

"As I was saying"—Ignoring the bloodbath that's about to happen, Astara sighs—"Leo is actually not a bad guy. Annoying, yes, but not a bad guy."

"Are you preparing his eulogy? Cause he is about to die."

"Don't be silly." Rolling her eyes, she huffs. "My brother or Fenrir wouldn't have listened to what he has to say until it was too late. By getting you riled up enough to get physical, he got both their attention in a matter of minutes. Brilliant, if you ask me."

"Oh dear fates, you put him up to it!" My mouth hangs open as I stare at her.

"I know." Sniffing primly, she lifts her chin. "I'm too smart for my own good."

"Or for his..." I cringe when Zoltan sends the shifter flying into the wall with a punch to his chest.

I've been avoiding him for so long, my heart is trying to punch a hole in my chest from seeing his handsome face again. Even angry, he takes my breath away, his body moving fluidly like the killing machine he was born to be. My lips part as I watch him pounce on the wolf, keeping him on the floor. Fenrir is not far behind, the Fae contrasting with his platinum hair next to Zoltan's dark strands like some twisted yin and yang animation right before my eyes. I'm about to shove Astara away and go help the poor soul when the fists stop flying and I see the vampire leaning closer to Leo, as Astara called him. Zoltan's head